MINI PONY COLLECTOR'S GUIDE

L B

Little, Brown and Company

New York Boston

CONTENTS

BLIND BAGS

EXCLUSIVES AND SETS

The enchanted lands of Equestria are filled with Unicorns, Pegasi, Earth Ponies, and other fantastical creatures. Inside this book, you'll find your favorite characters and discover new ones! Use the handy checklists to keep track of your mini pony collection as it grows.

BLiND BAG

PONY CHECKLIST

- ☐ Pinkie Pie
- ☐ Applejack
- ☐ Rainbow Dash
- ☐ Rarity
- ☐ Twilight Sparkle
- ☐ Fluttershy
- ☐ Sugar Grape
- ☐ Lily Blossom
- ☐ Minty
- ☐ Bumblesweet
- ☐ Fizzypop

- ☐ Flower Wishes
- ☐ Roseluck
- ☐ Sweetie Blue
- ☐ Pepperdance
- ☐ Lemon Hearts
- ☐ Cherry Spices
- ☐ Sweetie Swirl
- ☐ Lucky Swirl
- ☐ Sweetcream Scoops
- ☐ Firecracker Burst
- ☐ Pinkie Pie
  Crystal-Glitter
- ☐ Twilight Sparkle
  Crystal-Glitter
- ☐ Rainbow Dash
  Crystal-Glitter

4

Name

Pinkie Pie

Description

Pinkie Pie keeps her pony friends laughing and smiling all day! Cheerful and playful, she always looks on the bright side.

PINKIE PIE keeps her pony friends laughing and smiling all day! Cheerful and playful, she always looks on the bright side.

Eye Color
Blue

Hair Color
Dark Pink

Cutie Mark
Three Balloons

Color
Pink

Figure Style
Classic

Pony Tribe
Earth

Hair Color
Yellow

Eye Color
Green

Color
Orange

Cutie Mark
Three Apples

Pony Tribe
Earth

Figure Style
Classic

Figure 2

NAME

APPLEJACK

DESCRIPTION

Applejack is honest, friendly and sweet to the core! She loves to be outside, and her friends know they can always count on her.

TRADING CARD

my LITTLE PONY

APPLEJACK

APPLEJACK is honest, friendly and sweet to the core! She loves to be outside, and her friends know they can always count on her.

Name

RAINBOW DASH

Description

Rainbow Dash loves to fly as fast as she can! She is always ready to play a game, go on an adventure, or help out one of her friends.

TRADING CARD

Eye Color
Pink

Pony Tribe
Pegasus

Hair Color
Rainbow

Color
Blue

Cutie Mark
Rainbow
Lightning Bolt

Figure Style
Classic

Pony Tribe
Unicorn

Hair Color
Pink and Purple

Cutie Mark
Three Gems

Eye Color
Blue

Color
White

Figure Style
Classic

US Wave
2011 / 1

Figure
4

NAME

RARITY

DESCRIPTION

Rarity knows how to add sparkle to any outfit! She loves to give her friends advice on the latest pony fashions and hairstyles.

TRADING CARD

MY LITTLE PONY

RARITY knows how to add sparkle to any outfit! She loves to give her friends advice on the latest pony fashions and hairstyles.

Rarity

Hasbro

Hasbro

NAME

TWILIGHT SPARKLE

DESCRIPTION

Twilight Sparkle tries to find the answer to every question! Whether studying a book or spending time with friends, she always learns something new!

Eye Color
Purple

Pony Tribe
Unicorn

Cutie Mark
Pink Sparkle

Color
Purple

Figure Style
Classic

Hair Color
Pink and Purple

Hair Color
Pink

Eye Color
Green

Pony Tribe
Pegasus

Cutie Mark
Three Butterflies

Color
Yellow

Figure Style
Classic

NAME

FLUTTERSHY

DESCRIPTION

Fluttershy is a kind and gentle pony with a big heart. She likes to take care of others, especially her little animal friends!

TRADING CARD

MY LITTLE PONY

FLUTTERSHY
is a kind and gentle pony with a big heart. She likes to take care of others, especially her little animal friends!

Fluttershy

Hasbro

Hasbro

6

11

NAME

SUGAR GRAPE

DESCRIPTION

Sugar Grape loves to read stories. Fairy tales are her favorite!

TRADING CARD

Eye Color
Purple

Hair Color
Light and
Dark Purple

Pony Tribe
Pegasus

Figure Style
Classic

Cutie Mark
Bunch of Purple
Grapes

Color
White

Hair Color
Yellow

Eye Color
Purple

Pony Tribe
Pegasus

Cutie Mark
Lily

Color
Purple

Figure Style
Classic

TRADING CARD

NAME

LILY BLOSSOM

DESCRIPTION

Lily Blossom is known for being graceful when she flies, but she is just as elegant on all four hooves!

my LITTLE PONY

LILY BLOSSOM
is known for being graceful when she flies, but she is just as elegant on all four hooves!

LILY
BLOSSOM™

Hasbro

8

NAME

MINTY

DESCRIPTION

Minty loves to celebrate holidays with her friends! Her favorite season is winter.

TRADING CARD

MINTY®

MINTY loves to celebrate holidays with her friends! Her favorite season is winter.

Hair Color
Pink and White

Eye Color
Green

Color
Green

Cutie Mark
Three Mints

Figure Style
Classic

Pony Tribe
Earth

14

Hair Color
Orange and Yellow

Color
Orange

Eye Color
Blue

Cutie Mark
Bee

Pony Tribe
Earth

Figure Style
Classic

TRADING CARD

US Wave
2011 / 1

Figure
10

NAME

BUMBLESWEET

DESCRIPTION

Bumblesweet is very polite! She loves to talk to everypony and always has something nice to say.

15

NAME

FIZZYPOP

DESCRIPTION

Fizzypop loves to blow
bubbles as big as she can, but
her favorite part is watching
them pop!

TRADING CARD

Hair Color
Red and Pink

Eye Color
Blue

Figure Style
Classic

Pony Tribe
Earth

Cutie Mark
Sundae with Straw

Color
Purple

Hair Color
Green and White

Eye Color
Green

Figure Style
Classic

Cutie Mark
Two White Flowers

Color
Pink

Pony Tribe
Earth

NAME

FLOWER WISHES

DESCRIPTION

Flower Wishes has a beautiful garden. She grows flowers in every color of the rainbow!

TRADING CARD

MY LITTLE PONY

FLOWER WISHES
has a beautiful garden. She grows flowers in every color of the rainbow!

FLOWER WISHES

Hasbro

Hasbro

17

NAME

ROSELUCK

DESCRIPTION

Roseluck loves to pick pretty flowers and wear them in her hair!

TRADING CARD

ROSELUCK loves to pick pretty flowers and wear them in her hair!

Eye Color
Green

Figure Style
Classic

Hair Color
Pink and Red

Color
Yellow

Cutie Mark
Rose

Pony Tribe
Earth

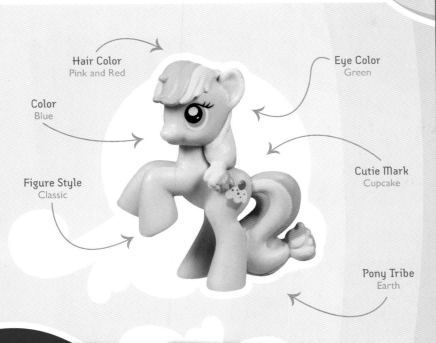

Hair Color
Pink and Red

Eye Color
Green

Color
Blue

Cutie Mark
Cupcake

Figure Style
Classic

Pony Tribe
Earth

US Wave
2011 / 1

Figure
14

NAME

SWEETIE BLUE

DESCRIPTION

Sweetie Blue loves to decorate sweet treats with sprinkles and fun toppings!

TRADING CARD

SWEETIE BLUE
loves to decorate sweet treats with sprinkles and fun toppings!

NAME

PEPPERDANCE

DESCRIPTION

Pepperdance loves to race with her friends! She is always ready for a challenge.

TRADING CARD

Eye Color
Green

Hair Color
Light and Dark Orange

Color
Red

Cutie Mark
Three Chili Peppers

Figure Style
Classic

Pony Tribe
Earth

Pony Tribe
Unicorn

Cutie Mark
Three Hearts

Hair Color
Blue

Eye Color
Purple

Color
Yellow

Figure Style
Classic

LEMON HEARTS
is loving and kind! She always
takes time to show her
friends how much she cares.

16

Name

LEMON HEARTS

DESCRIPTION

Lemon Hearts is loving and
kind! She always takes time to
show her friends how much
she cares.

US Wave
2011 / 1

Figure
17

Name

Cherry Spices

Description

Cherry Spices loves to bake treats! She makes up her own yummy recipes!

TRADING CARD

CHERRY SPICES
loves to bake treats!
She makes up her own
yummy recipes!

Hair Color
Pink and Red

Pony Tribe
Unicorn

Eye Color
Green

Cutie Mark
Two Cherries

Figure Style
Classic

Color
Brown

22

Hair Color
Pink, Yellow, and Blue

Pony Tribe
Unicorn

Eye Color
Green

Cutie Mark
Swirl Ice-Cream Cone

Figure Style
Classic

Color
Pink

US Wave
2011 / 1

Figure
18

NAME

Sweetie Swirl

DESCRIPTION

Sweetie Swirl loves ice cream!
Instead of choosing between
two flavors, she swirls them
together.

TRADING CARD

my LITTLE PONY

SWEETIE SWIRL

loves ice cream! Instead of
choosing between two flavors,
she swirls them together.

SWEETIE SWIRL

Hasbro

18

Name

Lucky Swirl

Description

Lucky Swirl loves playing games! No matter if she wins or loses, she always has fun!

Pony Tribe
Unicorn

Eye Color
Purple

Cutie Mark
Two Horseshoes

Color
Pink

Figure Style
Classic

Hair Color
Pink, Red, and Purple

24

Pony Tribe
Unicorn

Figure Style
Classic

Cutie Mark
Ice-Cream Cone

Eye Color
Blue

Color
Green

Hair Color
Orange, Yellow,
and Pink

NAME

SWEETCREAM SCOOPS

DESCRIPTION

Sweetcream Scoops loves to sing more than anything! She can even reach the really high notes!

TRADING CARD

MY LITTLE PONY

SWEETCREAM SCOOPS loves to sing more than anything! She can even reach the really high notes!

SWEETCREAM SCOOPS

Hasbro

Hasbro

20

US Wave
2011 / 1

Figure
21

NAME

FIRECRACKER BURST

DESCRIPTION

Firecracker Burst loves watching fireworks and guessing how they'll look when they burst—it's always a surprise!

TRADING CARD

Hair Color
Orange and Yellow

Pony Tribe
Unicorn

Eye Color
Blue

Color
Blue

Cutie Mark
Flame

Figure Style
Classic

Eye Color
Blue

Hair Color
Pink with Glitter

Color
Pink with Glitter

Cutie Mark
Three Balloons

Figure Style
Crystal-Glitter

Pony Tribe
Earth

NAME

PINKIE PIE

DESCRIPTION

Pinkie Pie keeps her pony friends laughing and smiling all day! Cheerful and playful, she always looks on the bright side.

TRADING CARD

MY LITTLE PONY

SPECIAL EDITION!

Pinkie Pie

Hasbro

PINKIE PIE keeps her pony friends laughing and smiling all day! Cheerful and playful, she always looks on the bright side.

SPECIAL EDITION!

Hasbro

22

Name

Twilight Sparkle

Description

Twilight Sparkle tries to find the answer to every question! Whether studying a book or spending time with friends, she always learns something new!

Eye Color
Purple

Pony Tribe
Unicorn

Cutie Mark
Pink Sparkle

Figure Style
Crystal-Glitter

Color
Purple with Glitter

Hair Color
Purple with Glitter

Figure Style
Crystal-Glitter

Pony Tribe
Pegasus

Hair Color
Blue with Glitter

Eye Color
Pink

Color
Blue with Glitter

Cutie Mark
Rainbow Lightning Bolt

NAME

RAINBOW DASH

DESCRIPTION

Rainbow Dash loves to fly as fast as she can! She is always ready to play a game, go on an adventure, or help out one of her friends.

TRADING CARD

my LITTLE PONY

RAINBOW DASH
loves to fly as fast as she can! She is always ready to play a game, go on an adventure, or help out one of her friends.

SPECIAL EDITION!

Rainbow Dash

Hasbro

SPECIAL EDITION!

Hasbro

BLIND BAG

PONY CHECKLIST

- ☐ Twilight Sparkle
- ☐ Rarity
- ☐ Bitta Luck
- ☐ Rainbowshine
- ☐ Goldengrape
- ☐ Pinkie Pie
  Glow-in-the-Dark
- ☐ Rainbow Dash
- ☐ Golden Harvest
- ☐ Sprinkle Stripe
- ☐ Sea Swirl
- ☐ Big McIntosh

- ☐ Twilight Sparkle
  Glow-in-the-Dark
- ☐ Pinkie Pie
- ☐ Apple Dazzle
- ☐ Lovestruck
- ☐ Berryshine
- ☐ Meadow Song
- ☐ Rarity
  Glow-in-the-Dark
- ☐ Applejack
- ☐ Fluttershy
- ☐ Cherry Berry
- ☐ Lyra Heartstrings
- ☐ Noteworthy
- ☐ Lucky Dreams

US Wave
2012 / 1

Figure
1

NAME

Twilight Sparkle

DESCRIPTION

Twilight Sparkle loves learning with her friends!

TRADING CARD

TWILIGHT SPARKLE

loves learning with her friends!

1

Pony Tribe
Unicorn

Eye Color
Purple

Cutie Mark
Pink Sparkle

Color
Purple

Hair Color
Pink and Purple

Figure Style
Classic

WWW.MYLITTLEPONY.COM

32

Hair Color
Pink and Purple

Pony Tribe
Unicorn

Eye Color
Blue

Cutie Mark
Three Gems

Color
White

Figure Style
Classic

US Wave
2012 / 1

Figure
2

NAME

RARITY

DESCRIPTION

Rarity gives her friends
great advice!

TRADING CARD

RARITY

gives her friends
great advice!

2

my little PONY

WWW.MYLITTLEPONY.COM

Name

Bitta Luck

Description

Bitta Luck is always busy
trying something new!

Eye Color
Purple

Hair Color
Pink and Light Purple

Pony Tribe
Earth

Cutie Mark
Ladybug

Color
Green

Figure Style
Classic

Hair Color
Pink

Eye Color
Pink

Pony Tribe
Pegasus

Color
Purple

Figure Style
Classic

Cutie Mark
Rainbow

US Wave
2012 / 1

Figure
4

NAME

RAINBOWSHINE

DESCRIPTION

Rainbowshine loves to leap
into the sky!

TRADING CARD

RAINBOWSHINE

loves to leap
into the sky!

MY LITTLE PONY

WWW.MYLITTLEPONY.COM

US Wave
2012 / 1

Figure
5

Name

GOLDENGRAPE

Description

Goldengrape loves telling and
hearing jokes.

TRADING CARD

GOLDENGRAPE

loves telling
and hearing jokes.

5

WWW.MYLITTLEPONY.COM

Eye Color
Blue

Hair Color
Purple

Cutie Mark
Two Bunches of
Green Grapes

Color
Yellow

Figure Style
Classic

Pony Tribe
Earth

Hair Color
Pink

Eye Color
Pink

Figure Style
Glow-in-the-Dark

Cutie Mark
Three Balloons

Color
Pink

Pony Tribe
Earth

NAME

PINKIE PIE

DESCRIPTION

Pinkie Pie keeps her friends laughing!

TRADING CARD

PINKIE PIE

keeps her friends laughing!

6

LYRA HEARTSTRINGS   FLUTTERSHY   WHITEWATER

LUCKY DREAMS   APPLEJACK   CHERRY BERRY

my LITTLE PONY

WWW.MYLITTLEPONY.COM

37

Figure
7

NAME

RAINBOW DASH

DESCRIPTION

Rainbow Dash loves to help her friends!

TRADING CARD

Figure Style
Classic

Eye Color
Purple

Pony Tribe
Pegasus

Color
Blue

Hair Color
Rainbow

Cutie Mark
Rainbow Lightning Bolt

Eye Color
Green

Hair Color
Orange

Cutie Mark
Two Carrots

Figure Style
Classic

Color
Yellow

Pony Tribe
Earth

NAME

GOLDEN HARVEST

DESCRIPTION

Golden Harvest loves sharing treats from the garden!

TRADING CARD

GOLDEN HARVEST

loves sharing treats
from the garden!

8

my LITTLE PONY

WWW.MYLITTLEPONY.COM

NAME

SPRINKLE STRIPE

DESCRIPTION

Sprinkle Stripe loves to have sweets for dessert!

TRADING CARD

Hair Color
White and Pink

Eye Color
Blue

Color
Pink

Cutie Mark
Cupcake

Pony Tribe
Earth

Figure Style
Classic

40

Pony Tribe
Unicorn

Cutie Mark
Two Dolphins

Eye Color
Pink

Color
Purple

Hair Color
Purple

Figure Style
Classic

Name

SEA SWIRL

Description

Sea Swirl loves to go
swimming in the ocean!

TRADING CARD

SEA SWIRL

loves to go swimming
in the ocean!

10

my LITTLE PONY

www.mylittlepony.com

41

US Wave
2012 / 1

Figure
11

Name

Big McIntosh

Description

Big McIntosh is very gentle
and wise.

TRADING CARD

BIG MCINTOSH

is very gentle
and wise.

11

my LITTLE PONY

WWW.MYLITTLEPONY.COM

Hair Color
Light Orange

Eye Color
Green

Cutie Mark
Green Apple

Figure Style
Classic

Pony Tribe
Earth

Color
Red

Pony Tribe
Unicorn

Eye Color
Purple

Cutie Mark
Pink Sparkle

Color
Purple

Hair Color
Purple

Figure Style
Glow-in-the-Dark

US Wave
2012 / 1

Figure
12

NAME

TWILIGHT SPARKLE

DESCRIPTION

Twilight Sparkle loves learning with her friends!

TRADING CARD

MY LITTLE PONY

TWILIGHT SPARKLE

loves learning with
her friends!

12

WWW.MYLITTLEPONY.COM

43

NAME

PINKIE PIE

DESCRIPTION

Pinkie Pie keeps her friends laughing!

Hair Color
Dark Pink

Eye Color
Blue

Cutie Mark
Three Balloons

Figure Style
Classic

Pony Tribe
Earth

Color
Pink

Eye Color
Purple

Color
Yellow

Figure Style
Classic

Hair Color
Pink and Red

Cutie Mark
Three Caramel Apples

Pony Tribe
Earth

NAME

APPLE DAZZLE

DESCRIPTION

Apple Dazzle is so loyal to
her friends!

TRADING CARD

APPLE DAZZLE™

is so loyal
to her friends!

14

GOLDEN HARVEST · SPARKLE STRIPE · BIG MCINTOSH
SEA SWIRL · AZURE RAGE · TWILIGHT SPARKLE

WWW.MYLITTLEPONY.COM

NAME

LOVESTRUCK

DESCRIPTION

Lovestruck loves watching and playing sports!

Pony Tribe
Unicorn

Eye Color
Green

Cutie Mark
Bow and Arrow

Color
White

Figure Style
Classic

Hair Color
Pink

Cutie Mark
Berries

Eye Color
Green

Color
Purple

Hair Color
Purple

Pony Tribe
Unicorn

Figure Style
Classic

US Wave
2012 / I

Figure
16

NAME

BERRYSHINE

DESCRIPTION

Berryshine loves berries more
than anypony!

TRADING CARD

BERRYSHINE™

loves berries
more than anypony!

16

my LITTLE PONY

WILDER SWEET   SPARKLE STRIPE   BIG MCINTOSH

SEA SWIRL   RAINBOW DASH   TWILIGHT SPARKLE

WWW.MYLITTLEPONY.COM

47

US Wave
2012 / 1

Figure
17

NAME

MEADOW SONG

DESCRIPTION

Meadow Song is so musical
and friendly!

TRADING CARD

MEADOW SONG

is so musical
and friendly!

17

Hasbro

Eye Color
Blue

Hair Color
Yellow

Cutie Mark
Guitar

Color
Brown

Pony Tribe
Earth

Figure Style
Classic

48

Cutie Mark
Three Gems

Pony Tribe
Unicorn

Hair Color
Fluorescent Green

Eye Color
Blue

Color
Fluorescent Green

Figure Style
Glow-in-the-Dark

US Wave
2012 / 1

Figure
18

NAME

RARITY

DESCRIPTION

Rarity gives her friends great advice!

TRADING CARD

RARITY

gives her friends
great advice!

18

MY LITTLE PONY

WWW.MYLITTLEPONY.COM

Figure
19

NAME

APPLEJACK

DESCRIPTION

Applejack is honest, friendly
and sweet to the core!

Eye Color
Green

Hair Color
Yellow

Color
Orange

Cutie Mark
Three Apples

Figure Style
Classic

Pony Tribe
Earth

TRADING CARD

APPLEJACK™
is honest, friendly and
sweet to the core!

19

Hasbro

WWW.MYLITTLEPONY.COM

Hasbro

Hair Color
Pink

Eye Color
Green

Pony Tribe
Pegasus

Color
Yellow

Figure Style
Classic

Cutie Mark
Three Butterflies

NAME

FLUTTERSHY

DESCRIPTION

Fluttershy likes taking care of her friends!

TRADING CARD

FLUTTERSHY

likes taking care of her friends!

20

MY LITTLE PONY

WWW.MYLITTLEPONY.COM

US Wave
2012 / 1

Figure
21

Name

CHERRY BERRY

Description

Cherry Berry is so cheerful all the time!

Hair Color
Yellow

Eye Color
Green

Cutie Mark
Two Cherries

Pony Tribe
Earth

Figure Style
Classic

Color
Pink

Pony Tribe
Unicorn

Color
Teal

Figure Style
Classic

Eye Color
Orange

Cutie Mark
Harp

Hair Color
Light Teal

US Wave
2012 / 1

Figure
22

NAME

LYRA HEARTSTRINGS

DESCRIPTION

Lyra Heartstrings sings and plays all day!

TRADING CARD

LYRA HEARTSTRINGS

sings and plays all day!

22

Hasbro

my LITTLE PONY

Hasbro

WWW.MYLITTLEPONY.COM

Figure
23

Name

NOTEWORTHY

Description

Noteworthy is very helpful and remembers everything!

TRADING CARD

NOTEWORTHY

is very helpful and remembers everything!

23

Eye Color
Blue

Hair Color
Dark Blue

Cutie Mark
Three Musical Notes

Color
Blue

Pony Tribe
Earth

Figure Style
Classic

54

Hair Color
Pink and Blue

Eye Color
Green

Pony Tribe
Pegasus

Color
Green

Figure Style
Classic

Cutie Mark
Horseshoe and Hearts

NAME

LUCKY DREAMS

DESCRIPTION

Lucky Dreams is just so lucky all the time!

TRADING CARD

LUCKY DREAMS

is just so lucky
all the time!

24

my LITTLE PONY

WWW.MYLITTLEPONY.COM

BLIND BAG

PONY CHECKLIST

- ☐ Applejack
- ☐ Fluttershy
- ☐ Trixie Lulamoon
- ☐ Crimson Gala
- ☐ Minuette
- ☐ Royal Riff
- ☐ Pinkie Pie
- ☐ Merry May
- ☐ Electric Sky
- ☐ Chance-A-Lot
- ☐ Berry Green
- ☐ Rarity
  Metallic-Shimmer

- ☐ Twilight Sparkle
- ☐ Rarity
- ☐ Sassaflash
- ☐ Peachy Sweet
- ☐ Twilight Sky
- ☐ Applejack
  Metallic-Shimmer
- ☐ Rainbow Dash
- ☐ Mosely Orange
- ☐ Amethyst Star
- ☐ Twilight Velvet
- ☐ Shoeshine
- ☐ Pinkie Pie
  Metallic-Shimmer

NAME

APPLEJACK

DESCRIPTION

Applejack is honest, friendly
and sweet to the core!

Eye Color
Green

Hair Color
Orange with
Glitter

Color
Orange with
Glitter

Cutie Mark
Three Apples

Figure Style
Crystal-Glitter

Pony Tribe
Earth

Hair Color
Yellow with Glitter

Pony Tribe
Pegasus

Color
Yellow with Glitter

Eye Color
Green

Figure Style
Crystal-Glitter

Cutie Mark
Three Butterflies

NAME

FLUTTERSHY

DESCRIPTION

Fluttershy likes taking care of her friends!

TRADING CARD

FLUTTERSHY
likes taking care of her friends!

2

my LITTLE PONY

BEAUTY   ELECTRIC SKY   PINKIE PIE

MERRY MAY   CHANCE-A-LOT   BERRY GREEN

WWW.MYLITTLEPONY.COM

59

NAME

TRIXIE LULAMOON

DESCRIPTION

Trixie Lulamoon is great at magic tricks!

TRADING CARD

TRIXIE LULAMOON

is great at magic tricks!

3

Hair Color
Blue with Glitter

Pony Tribe
Unicorn

Cutie Mark
Wand and Moon

Eye Color
Purple

Figure Style
Crystal-Glitter

Color
Blue with Glitter

my LITTLE PONY

RARITY

ELECTRIC SKY

PINKIE PIE

BERRY WAY

CHANCE-A-LOT

BERRY GREEN

WWW.MYLITTLEPONY.COM

Hair Color
Pink with Glitter

Eye Color
Green

Pony Tribe
Earth

Figure Style
Crystal-Glitter

Cutie Mark
Three Cupcakes

Color
Pink with Glitter

US Wave
2012 / 2

Figure
4

NAME

CRIMSON GALA

DESCRIPTION

Crimson Gala gives everyone treats when she visits!

TRADING CARD

CRIMSON GALA

gives everyone treats when she visits!

4

My LITTLE PONY

ARITY   ELECTRIC SKY   PINKIE ME

MERRY MAY   CHANCE-A-LOT   BERRY GREEN

WWW.MYLITTLEPONY.COM

NAME

MiNUETTE

DESCRIPTION

Minuette is always on time
with the help of some magic!

TRADING CARD

MiNUETTE

is always on time
with the help
of some magic!

5

my LiTTLE PONY

RARITY   ELECTRIC SKY   PINKIE PIE

MERRY MAY   CHANCE-A-LOT   BERRY GREEN

WWW.MYLITTLEPONY.COM

Pony Tribe
Unicorn

Hair Color
Blue with Glitter

Eye Color
Blue

Cutie Mark
Hourglass

Color
Blue with Glitter

Figure Style
Crystal-Glitter

Color
Purple with Glitter

Eye Color
Orange

Cutie Mark
Two Treble Clefs

Hair Color
Purple with Glitter

Figure Style
Crystal-Glitter

Pony Tribe
Earth

NAME

ROYAL RIFF

DESCRIPTION

Royal Riff makes up songs to sing together with friends!

TRADING CARD

ROYAL RIFF

makes up songs to sing together with friends!

Hasbro

6

RARITY

ELECTRIC SKY

PINKIE PIE

MERRY MAY

CHANCE-A-LOT

BERRY GREEN

My LITTLE PONY

Hasbro

WWW.MYLITTLEPONY.COM

NAME

PINKIE PIE

DESCRIPTION

Pinkie Pie keeps her friends laughing and smiling all day!

TRADING CARD

Hair Color
Pink with Glitter

Cutie Mark
Three Balloons

Eye Color
Blue

Color
Pink with Glitter

Pony Tribe
Earth

Figure Style
Crystal-Glitter

Hair Color
Green with Glitter

Pony Tribe
Pegasus

Figure Style
Crystal-Glitter

Eye Color
Pink

Color
Green with Glitter

Cutie Mark
Three Flowers

NAME

MERRY MAY

DESCRIPTION

Merry May loves all flowers, especially spring daisies!

TRADING CARD

MERRY MAY™

loves all flowers, especially spring daisies!

8

my LITTLE **PONY**

TRIXIE LULAMOON · APPLEJACK · CRIMSON GALA

FLITTERBERRY · ROYAL RIFF · MIGUETTE

WWW.MYLITTLEPONY.COM

NAME

ELECTRIC SKY

DESCRIPTION

Electric Sky has so many
smart ideas to share!

TRADING CARD

ELECTRIC SKY™

has so many smart
ideas to share!

9

Pony Tribe
Unicorn

Hair Color
Yellow with
Glitter

Eye Color
Blue

Color
Yellow with
Glitter

Cutie Mark
Three Lightbulbs

Figure Style
Crystal-Glitter

WWW.MYLITTLEPONY.COM

Eye Color
Blue

Cutie Mark
Three Horseshoes

Hair Color
Orange with
Glitter

Color
Orange with
Glitter

Figure Style
Crystal-Glitter

Pony Tribe
Earth

US Wave
2012 / 2

Figure
10

NAME

CHANCE-A-LOT

DESCRIPTION

Chance-A-Lot is always
cheerful and trying new things!

TRADING
CARD

CHANCE-A-LOT

is always cheerful
and trying new things!

10

MY LITTLE
PONY

PRAIRIE LULAMOON   APPLEJACK   CRIMSON GALA

FLUTTERSHY   ROYAL RIFF   MINUETTE

WWW.MYLITTLEPONY.COM

NAME

BERRY GREEN

DESCRIPTION

Berry Green has lots of friends she can always count on!

TRADING CARD

BERRY GREEN

has lots of friends
she can always count on!

11

my LITTLE PONY

TRIXIE LULAMOON   APPLEJACK   CRIMSON GALA

FLUTTERSHY   ROYAL RIFF   MINUETTE

WWW.MYLITTLEPONY.COM

Hair Color
Pink with
Glitter

Eye Color
Green

Color
Pink with
Glitter

Figure Style
Crystal-Glitter

Cutie Mark
Two Bunches of
Green Grapes

Pony Tribe
Earth

Pony Tribe
Unicorn

Eye Color
Blue

Cutie Mark
Three Gems

Color
Silver Metallic

Hair Color
Silver Metallic

Figure Style
Metallic-Shimmer

US Wave
2012 / 2

Figure
12

NAME

RARITY

DESCRIPTION

Rarity loves to give her
friends great advice!

TRADING CARD

RARITY

loves to give her
friends great advice!

Hasbro

12

TWILIGHT SPARKLE   APPLEJACK   RAINBOW DASH

FLUTTERSHY   ROYAL RIFF   MINUETTE

My LITTLE PONY

Hasbro

WWW.MYLITTLEPONY.COM

NAME

TWILIGHT SPARKLE

DESCRIPTION

Twilight Sparkle loves learning with her friends!

TRADING CARD

TWILIGHT SPARKLE

loves learning with her friends!

Hasbro

13

MY LITTLE PONY

AMETHYST STAR   TWILIGHT VELVET   MINNIE PIE

RAINBOW DASH   MOSELY ORANGE   SUNSHINE

Hasbro

WWW.MYLITTLEPONY.COM

Pony Tribe
Unicorn

Eye Color
Purple

Color
Purple with Glitter

Hair Color
Purple with Glitter

Cutie Mark
Pink Sparkle

Figure Style
Crystal-Glitter

70

Hair Color
White with Glitter

Pony Tribe
Unicorn

Cutie Mark
Three Gems

Eye Color
Blue

Color
White with Glitter

Figure Style
Crystal-Glitter

US Wave 2012 / 2

Figure 14

NAME

RARITY

DESCRIPTION

Rarity loves to give her friends great advice!

Name

Sassaflash

Description

Sassaflash loves watching clouds blow across the sky!

TRADING CARD

Hair Color
Blue-Green
with Glitter

Eye Color
Orange

Pony Tribe
Pegasus

Color
Blue-Green
with Glitter

Figure Style
Crystal-Glitter

Cutie Mark
Two Lightning Bolts

72

Hair Color
Green with Glitter

Color
Green with Glitter

Pony Tribe
Earth

Eye Color
Green

Cutie Mark
Pie

Figure Style
Crystal-Glitter

US Wave 2012 / 2

Figure 16

NAME

PEACHY SWEET

DESCRIPTION

Peachy Sweet is always smiling wherever she goes!

TRADING CARD

PEACHY SWEET

is always smiling wherever she goes!

16

Hasbro

AMETHYST STAR

TWILIGHT VELVET

PONDIE PIE

RAINBOW DASH

MOSELY ORANGE

SUNSHINE

WWW.MYLITTLEPONY.COM

73

US Wave
2012 / 2

Figure
17

Name

Twilight Sky

Description

Twilight Sky loves to play
guessing games with friends!

TRADING CARD

TWILIGHT SKY

loves to play
guessing games with friends!

17

My Little Pony

AMETHYST STAR   TWILIGHT VELVET   PINKIE PIE

RAINBOW DASH

MOSELY ORANGE   SUNSHINE

WWW.MYLITTLEPONY.COM

Hair Color
Gray with
Glitter

Eye Color
Blue

Cutie Mark
Three Stars

Color
Gray with
Glitter

Figure Style
Crystal-Glitter

Pony Tribe
Earth

74

Eye Color
Green

Hair Color
Gold Metallic

Pony Tribe
Earth

Cutie Mark
Three Apples

Figure Style
Metallic-Shimmer

Color
Gold Metallic

Name

APPLEJACK

Description

Applejack is honest, friendly and sweet to the core!

APPLEJACK™

is honest, friendly
and sweet to the core!

Hasbro

18

AMETHYST STAR

TWILIGHT VELVET

PINKIE PIE

RAINBOW DASH

MOSELY ORANGE

CHERRIES

Hasbro

WWW.MYLITTLEPONY.COM

Name

RAINBOW DASH

Description

Rainbow Dash is always ready to help her friends.

TRADING CARD

RAINBOW DASH

is always ready to help her friends.

19

Hasbro

my LITTLE PONY

RARITY   APPLEJACK   PEACHY SWEET

RAINBOWDASH   TWILIGHT SKY   TWILIGHT SPARKLE

WWW.MYLITTLEPONY.COM

Hasbro

Hair Color
Blue with Glitter

Eye Color
Purple

Pony Tribe
Pegasus

Cutie Mark
Rainbow Lightning Bolt

Color
Blue with Glitter

Figure Style
Crystal-Glitter

76

Cutie Mark
Orange

Hair Color
Yellow with Glitter

Color
Yellow with Glitter

Eye Color
Blue

Figure Style
Crystal-Glitter

Pony Tribe
Earth

NAME

MOSELY ORANGE

DESCRIPTION

Mosely Orange loves to have fancy parties!

TRADING CARD

MOSELY ORANGE

loves to have fancy parties!

Hasbro

20

my LITTLE PONY

RARITY   APPLEJACK   PEACHY SWEET

SUGARCANE   TWILIGHT RAY   TWILIGHT SPARKLE

Hasbro

WWW.MYLITTLEPONY.COM

77

NAME

AMETHYST STAR

DESCRIPTION

Amethyst Star loves to dance when she hears music!

TRADING CARD

AMETHYST STAR

loves to dance
when she hears music!

21

Hasbro

RARITY   APPLEJACK   PEACHY SWEET

SASSAFLASH   TWILIGHT SKY   TWILIGHT SPARKLE

WWW.MYLITTLEPONY.COM

Hasbro

Hair Color
Pink with Glitter

Eye Color
Purple

Cutie Mark
Three Diamonds

Figure Style
Crystal-Glitter

Color
Pink with Glitter

Pony Tribe
Unicorn

Pony Tribe
Unicorn

Color
White with
Glitter

Figure Style
Crystal-Glitter

Eye Color
Blue

Cutie Mark
Three Stars

Hair Color
White with
Glitter

NAME

TWILIGHT VELVET

DESCRIPTION

Twilight Velvet loves writing
stories about adventures!

TRADING CARD

TWILIGHT VELVET
loves writing
stories about adventures!

22

RARITY   APPLEJACK   PEACHY SWEET

SAPHIRELASH   TWILIGHT SKY   TWILIGHT SPARKLE

WWW.MYLITTLEPONY.COM

NAME

SHOESHINE

DESCRIPTION

Shoeshine is understanding and listens to her friends!

TRADING CARD

SHOESHINE™
is understanding
and listens to her friends!

23

Hair Color
Blue with Glitter

Eye Color
Pink

Color
Blue with Glitter

Cutie Mark
Two Horseshoes

Figure Style
Crystal-Glitter

Pony Tribe
Earth

Hair Color
Pink Metallic

Color
Pink Metallic

Figure Style
Metallic-Shimmer

Eye Color
Blue

Cutie Mark
Three Balloons

Pony Tribe
Earth

NAME

PINKIE PIE

DESCRIPTION

Pinkie Pie keeps her friends laughing and smiling all day!

TRADING CARD

PINKIE PIE

keeps her friends laughing and smiling all day!

Hasbro

24

my LITTLE PONY

RARITY   APPLEJACK   PEACHY SWEET

SASSAFLASH   TWILIGHT SKY   TWILIGHT SPARKLE

Hasbro

WWW.MYLITTLEPONY.COM

BLiND BAG

PONY CHECKLIST

- ☐ Twilight Sparkle
- ☐ Princess Cadance
- ☐ Sunny Rays
- ☐ Junebug
- ☐ Breezie
- ☐ Island Rainbow
- ☐ Princess Luna
- ☐ Sapphire Shores
- ☐ Rainbow Dash
- ☐ Flippity Flop
- ☐ Gardenia Glow
- ☐ Skywishes

- ☐ Trixie Lulamoon
- ☐ Diamond Rose
- ☐ Cinnamon Breeze
- ☐ Ploomette
- ☐ Golden Delicious
- ☐ Ribbon Wishes
- ☐ Princess Celestia
- ☐ Fluttershy
- ☐ Forsythia
- ☐ Flitterheart
- ☐ Rainbow Wishes
- ☐ Lyra Heartstrings

NAME

TWILIGHT SPARKLE

DESCRIPTION

Twilight Sparkle loves learning with her friends!

Pony Tribe
Unicorn

Figure Style
Classic

Eye Color
Purple

Cutie Mark
Pink Sparkle

Color
Purple

Hair Color
Pink and Purple

84

Pony Tribe
Pegasus Unicorn

Eye Color
Purple

Color
Pink

Cutie Mark
Crystal Heart

Hair Color
Pink, Purple, and Yellow

Figure Style
Classic

US Wave
2012 / 3

Figure
2

NAME

PRINCESS CADANCE

DESCRIPTION

Princess Cadance likes to spend time helping others.

TRADING CARD

PRINCESS CADANCE™

likes to spend time helping others.

Hasbro

02

MY LITTLE PONY
FRIENDSHIP IS MAGIC

TWILIGHT SPARKLE™   PRINCESS CADANCE™   SUNNY RAYS™

ISLAND RAINBOW™   BREEZIE™   JUNEBUG™

WWW.MYLITTLEPONY.COM

NAME

SUNNY RAYS

DESCRIPTION

Sunny Rays has a lot of bright
ideas to share.

SUNNY RAYS™

has a lot of bright
ideas to share.

03

MY LITTLE PONY
FRIENDSHIP IS MAGIC

TWILIGHT SPARKLE™   PRINCESS CADENCE™   SUNNY RAYS™

ISLAND RAINBOW™   BREEZIE™   JUNEBUG™

WWW.MYLITTLEPONY.COM

Hair Color
Pink

Eye Color
Purple

Pony Tribe
Pegasus

Color
Yellow

Cutie Mark
Three Suns

Figure Style
Classic

Pony Tribe
Unicorn

Eye Color
Green

Cutie Mark
June Bug

Color
Pink

Hair Color
Yellow

Figure Style
Classic

US Wave
2012 / 3

Figure
4

Name

JUNEBUG

Description

Junebug loves to celebrate holidays with friends!

TRADING CARD

JUNEBUG™

loves to celebrate holidays with friends!

04

Hasbro

My Little Pony
FRIENDSHIP IS MAGIC

TWILIGHT SPARKLE™   PRINCESS CADANCE™   SUNNY RAYS™

ISLAND RAINBOW™   BREEZIE™   JUNEBUG™

WWW.MYLITTLEPONY.COM

87

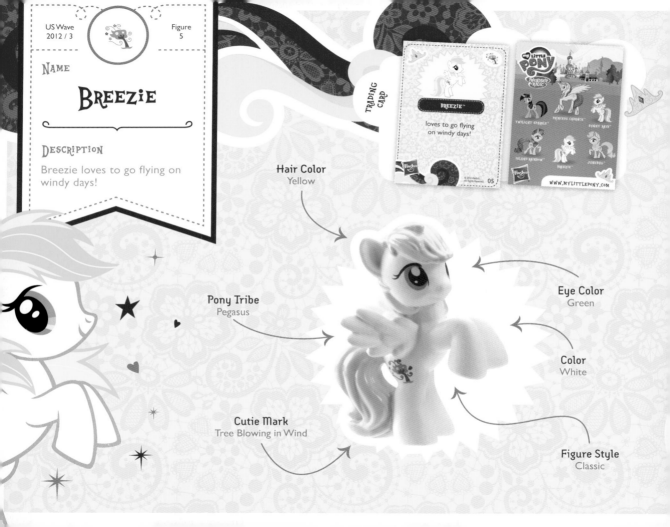

US Wave
2012 / 3

Figure
5

NAME

BREEZIE

DESCRIPTION

Breezie loves to go flying on windy days!

Hair Color
Yellow

Eye Color
Green

Pony Tribe
Pegasus

Color
White

Cutie Mark
Tree Blowing in Wind

Figure Style
Classic

Pony Tribe
Unicorn

Eye Color
Blue

Cutie Mark
Island, Palm Tree,
and Rainbow

Color
Pink

Hair Color
Pink

Figure Style
Classic

NAME

ISLAND
RAINBOW

DESCRIPTION

Island Rainbow loves to go to
the beach and relax!

TRADING CARD

ISLAND RAINBOW™
loves to go to
the beach and relax!

MY LITTLE PONY
FRIENDSHIP IS MAGIC

TWILIGHT SPARKLE™   PRINCESS CADENCE™   SUNNY RAYS™

ISLAND RAINBOW™   RARIETA™   SUNSPOT™

WWW.MYLITTLEPONY.COM

89

NAME

PRINCESS LUNA

DESCRIPTION

Princess Luna stays up late to watch the stars!

TRADING CARD

PRINCESS LUNA™

stays up late
to watch the stars!

© 2012 Hasbro.
All Rights Reserved.

07

MY LITTLE PONY

FRIENDSHIP IS MAGIC

RAINBOW DASH™   PRINCESS LUNA™   CHEERILEE DOUBLES™

SKYWISHES™   CARAMEL APPLE™   FLIPPITY FLOP™

WWW.MYLITTLEPONY.COM

Pony Tribe
Pegasus Unicorn

Eye Color
Blue

Cutie Mark
Night Sky with
Moon and Stars

Color
Purple

Hair Color
Dark Pink, Blue,
and Purple

Figure Style
Classic

Pony Tribe
Unicorn

Eye Color
Blue

Color
Light Green

Cutie Mark
Seashell

Hair Color
Blue and White

Figure Style
Classic

NAME

SAPPHIRE SHORES

DESCRIPTION

Sapphire Shores loves to
collect pretty seashells.

TRADING CARD

SAPPHIRE SHORES

loves to collect
pretty seashells.

08

MY LITTLE PONY
FRIENDSHIP IS MAGIC

RAINBOW DASH   PRINCESS LUNA   SAPPHIRE SHORES

DAYBREAKER   GRANNY SMITH   FLUTTERSHY

WWW.MYLITTLEPONY.COM

91

NAME

RAINBOW DASH

DESCRIPTION

Rainbow Dash is always ready to help her friends.

Hair Color
Rainbow

Pony Tribe
Pegasus

Cutie Mark
Rainbow Lightning Bolt

Eye Color
Purple

Color
Blue

Figure Style
Classic

TRADING CARD

RAINBOW DASH™

is always ready
to help her friends.

09

my little PONY
FRIENDSHIP IS MAGIC

RAINBOW DASH™   PRINCESS LUNA™   SAPPHIRE SHORES™

DAYBREAKER™   GARDENIA GLOW™   FLUTTER FLAP™

WWW.MYLITTLEPONY.COM

Hair Color
Dark Pink

Pony Tribe
Unicorn

Cutie Mark
Flowered Flip-Flops

Eye Color
Blue

Color
Yellow

Figure Style
Classic

NAME

FLIPPITY FLOP

DESCRIPTION

Flippity Flop changes her mind
a lot, but always has fun!

TRADING CARD

FLIPPITY FLOP™

changes her mind
a lot, but
always has fun!

Hasbro   10

MY LITTLE PONY
FRIENDSHIP IS MAGIC

RAINBOW DASH™   PRINCESS LUNA™   SAPPHIRE SHORES™

DAYDREAM™   GARDENIA GLOW™   FLIPPITY FLOP™

WWW.MYLITTLEPONY.COM

93

NAME

GARDENIA GLOW

DESCRIPTION

Gardenia Glow knows how to make a garden grow!

GARDENIA GLOW

knows how to make
a garden grow!

Pony Tribe
Unicorn

Eye Color
Blue

Hair Color
Pink

Color
Blue

Cutie Mark
Flower

Figure Style
Classic

Pony Tribe
Pegasus

Eye Color
Green

Cutie Mark
Kite

Color
Pink

Hair Color
Pink

Figure Style
Classic

US Wave
2012 / 3

Figure
12

NAME

SKYWISHES

DESCRIPTION

Skywishes has big dreams and
never gives up!

TRADING CARD

SKYWISHES™

has big dreams
and never gives up!

12

Hasbro

MY LITTLE PONY
FRIENDSHIP IS MAGIC

RAINBOW DASH™   PRINCESS LUNA™   SAPPHIRE SHORES™

SKYWISHES™   GARDENIA GLOW™   FLIPPITY FLOP™

WWW.MYLITTLEPONY.COM

Name

Trixie Lulamoon

Description

Trixie Lulamoon is great at magic tricks!

Trixie Lulamoon

is great at magic tricks!

WWW.MYLITTLEPONY.COM

Pony Tribe
Unicorn

Eye Color
Purple

Color
Blue

Hair Color
Blue and White

Figure Style
Classic

Cutie Mark
Wand and Moon

Hair Color
Dark Pink

Eye Color
Blue

Pony Tribe
Pegasus

Color
White

Cutie Mark
Pink Diamond

Figure Style
Classic

NAME

DIAMOND ROSE

DESCRIPTION

Diamond Rose loves to give gifts to her friends!

DIAMOND ROSE

loves to give gifts to her friends!

Hasbro

© 2012 Hasbro.
All Rights Reserved.

14

MY LITTLE PONY
FRIENDSHIP IS MAGIC

CINNAMON BREEZE   DIAMOND ROSE   TWISTY SUGARRUSH

PLUMETTE   GOLDEN DELICIOUS   RIBBIE WISHES

WWW.MYLITTLEPONY.COM

NAME

CINNAMON BREEZE

DESCRIPTION

Cinnamon Breeze likes the smell of freshly baked treats!

Pony Tribe
Unicorn

Cutie Mark
Cinnamon Roll

Eye Color
Brown

Hair Color
Dark Pink

Color
Pink

Figure Style
Classic

98

Pony Tribe
Pegasus

Eye Color
Blue

Cutie Mark
Heart with Crown

Color
Pink

Hair Color
Yellow and Blue

Figure Style
Classic

US Wave
2012 / 3

Figure
16

NAME

PLOOMETTE

DESCRIPTION

Ploomette dreams of
becoming a princess someday!

TRADING CARD

PLOOMETTE™

dreams of becoming
a princess someday!

16

MY LITTLE PONY
FRIENDSHIP IS MAGIC

CINNAMON BREEZE™   DIAMOND ROSE™   THISTLE DREAMING™

PLOOMETTE™   GOLDEN PRINCESS™   MOSAIC WISHES™

WWW.MYLITTLEPONY.COM

NAME

GOLDEN DELICIOUS

DESCRIPTION

Golden Delicious loves acting like a movie star!

TRADING CARD

GOLDEN DELICIOUS

loves acting like a movie star!

17

my LITTLE PONY
FRIENDSHIP IS MAGIC

CHEERILEE BREEZIE   DIAMOND ROSE   TRIXIE LULAMOON

PLUMETTE   GOLDEN DELICIOUS   HYDEIA WISHES

WWW.MYLITTLEPONY.COM

Eye Color
Green

Pony Tribe
Unicorn

Cutie Mark
Apple in Heart

Color
Light Green

Hair Color
Yellow and Pink

Figure Style
Classic

Hair Color
Blue and Purple

Pony Tribe
Unicorn

Cutie Mark
Wand and Stars

Eye Color
Purple

US Wave
2012 / 3

Figure
18

NAME

RIBBON
WISHES

DESCRIPTION

Ribbon Wishes loves to wish
on shooting stars!

Color
Dark Pink

Figure Style
Classic

TRADING CARD

RIBBON WISHES™

loves to wish on
shooting stars!

18

MY LITTLE PONY
FRIENDSHIP IS MAGIC

CINNAMON BREEZE   DIAMOND ROSE   PIXIE SPLASHER

PLUMETTE   CHERRY DELICIOUS   RIBBON WISHES

Name

PRINCESS CELESTIA

Description

Princess Celestia is a magical and beautiful pony!

Pony Tribe
Pegasus Unicorn

Eye Color
Purple

Cutie Mark
Sun

Color
White

Hair Color
Pink, Green, and Blue

Figure Style
Classic

Hair Color
Pink

Eye Color
Green

Pony Tribe
Pegasus

Color
Yellow

Cutie Mark
Three Butterflies

Figure Style
Classic

US Wave
2012 / 3

Figure
20

NAME

FLUTTERSHY

DESCRIPTION

Fluttershy likes taking care of her friends!

TRADING CARD

FLUTTERSHY™

likes taking care of her friends!

20

WWW.MYLITTLEPONY.COM

103

Name

FORSYTHIA

DESCRIPTION

Forsythia loves to see spring flowers in bloom!

FORSYTHIA

loves to see spring flowers in bloom!

MY LITTLE PONY

FRIENDSHIP IS MAGIC

FLUTTERHEART   PRINCESS CELESTIA   LYRA HEARTSTRINGS

FORSYTHIA   RAINBOW WISHES   FLUTTERPONY

WWW.MYLITTLEPONY.COM

Hasbro

© 2012 Hasbro.
All Rights Reserved.   21

Eye Color
Blue

Pony Tribe
Unicorn

Cutie Mark
Forsythia and Butterfly

Color
Light Purple

Hair Color
Green

Figure Style
Classic

Hair Color
Blue and Purple

Eye Color
Blue

Pony Tribe
Pegasus

Color
Pink

Figure Style
Classic

Cutie Mark
Two Hearts

NAME

FLITTERHEART

DESCRIPTION

Flitterheart lets her dreams
soar as high as she can fly!

TRADING CARD

FLITTERHEART™

lets her dreams soar
as high as she can fly!

Hasbro

22

MY LITTLE PONY
FRIENDSHIP IS MAGIC

FLITTERHEART   PRINCESS CELESTIA   LYRA HEARTSTRINGS

SWEETPEA   RAINBOW WISHES   FLUTTERSHY

Hasbro

WWW.MYLITTLEPONY.COM

Name

RAINBOW WISHES

Description

Rainbow Wishes chases
rainbows across the sky!

RAINBOW WISHES™

chases rainbows
across the sky!

23

my little
PONY
RAINBOW
MAGIC

FLUTTERSHY™   PRINCESS CELESTIA™   LYRA HEARTSTRINGS™

PONYTAIL™   RAINBOW WISHES™   FLUTTERSHY™

WWW.MYLITTLEPONY.COM

Pony Tribe
Unicorn

Eye Color
Blue

Hair Color
Blue and Dark Pink

Cutie Mark
Star and Rainbow

Figure Style
Classic

Color
White

Pony Tribe
Unicorn

Eye Color
Orange

Hair Color
Light Teal and White

Cutie Mark
Harp

Color
Light Teal

Figure Style
Classic

NAME

LYRA HEARTSTRINGS

DESCRIPTION

Lyra Heartstrings sings and plays all day!

TRADING CARD

LYRA HEARTSTRINGS™

sings and plays
all day!

24

MY LITTLE PONY
FRIENDSHIP IS MAGIC

WWW.MYLITTLEPONY.COM

BLiND BAG

PONY CHECKLIST

- ☐ Pinkie Pie
- ☐ Fluttershy
- ☐ Twilight Sparkle
  Shimmer-Gem
- ☐ Rainbow Dash
- ☐ Rarity
- ☐ Applejack
- ☐ Minuette
- ☐ Roseluck
- ☐ Trixie Lulamoon
  Shimmer-Gem
- ☐ Twilight Velvet
  Shimmer-Gem

- ☐ Mosely Orange
- ☐ Berry Green
- ☐ Merry May
- ☐ Cherry Spices
- ☐ Electric Sky
- ☐ Crimson Gala
- ☐ Amethyst Star
- ☐ Twilight Sky
- ☐ Sassaflash
- ☐ Magnet Bolt
- ☐ Royal Riff
- ☐ Peachy Sweet
- ☐ Chance-A-Lot
- ☐ Shoeshine

NAME

PINKIE PIE

DESCRIPTION

Pinkie Pie keeps her friends laughing and smiling all day!

PINKIE PIE®

keeps her friends laughing
and smiling all day!

01

www.MYLITTLEPONY.COM

Hair Color
Dark Pink

Cutie Mark
Three Balloons

Eye Color
Blue

Pony Tribe
Earth

Color
Pink

Figure Style
Classic

Hair Color
Pink

Eye Color
Green

Pony Tribe
Pegasus

Cutie Mark
Three Butterflies

Color
Yellow

Figure Style
Classic

Name

FLUTTERSHY

Description

Fluttershy likes taking care of her friends!

TRADING CARD

FLUTTERSHY®

likes taking care
of her friends!

02

WWW.MYLITTLEPONY.COM

113

NAME

TWILIGHT SPARKLE

DESCRIPTION

Twilight Sparkle loves learning with her friends!

TWILIGHT SPARKLE™

loves learning with her friends!

03

WWW.MYLITTLEPONY.COM

Pony Tribe
Unicorn

Eye Color
Purple

Cutie Mark
Pink Sparkle

Hair Color
Pink and Purple

Color
Purple

Figure Style
Shimmer-Gem

Hair Color
Rainbow

Eye Color
Pink

Pony Tribe
Pegasus

Cutie Mark
Rainbow
Lightning Bolt

Color
Blue

Figure Style
Classic

NAME

RAINBOW DASH

DESCRIPTION

Rainbow Dash is always ready to help her friends!

TRADING CARD

RAINBOW DASH®

is always ready to help her friends.

my LITTLE PONY
FRIENDSHIP
MAGIC

WWW.MYLITTLEPONY.COM

04

Name

Rarity

Description

Rarity loves to give her friends great advice!

TRADING CARD

RARITY ®
loves to give her friends great advice!

05

my LITTLE PONY
FRIENDSHIP IS MAGIC

WWW.MYLITTLEPONY.COM

Hair Color
Pink and Purple

Pony Tribe
Unicorn

Cutie Mark
Three Gems

Eye Color
Blue

Color
White

Figure Style
Classic

Hair Color
Yellow

Eye Color
Green

Color
Orange

Cutie Mark
Three Apples

Pony Tribe
Earth

Figure Style
Classic

NAME

APPLEJACK

DESCRIPTION

Applejack is honest, friendly and sweet to the core!

TRADING CARD

APPLEJACK™

is honest, friendly and sweet to the core!

06

MY LITTLE PONY

FRIENDSHIP IS MAGIC

WWW.MYLITTLEPONY.COM

Name

MINUETTE

Description

Minuette is always on time with the help of some magic!

Pony Tribe
Unicorn

Trading Card

MINUETTE™

is always on time with the help of some magic!

07

WWW.MYLITTLEPONY.COM

Eye Color
Blue

Cutie Mark
Hourglass

Hair Color
Dark Blue

Color
Blue

Figure Style
Classic

116

Hair Color
Pink and Red

Eye Color
Green

Color
Yellow

Cutie Mark
Rose

Pony Tribe
Earth

Figure Style
Classic

US Wave
2013 / 1

Figure
8

Name

ROSELUCK

Description

Roseluck loves to pick pretty
flowers and wear them in her
hair!

TRADING
CARD

ROSELUCK™

loves to pick pretty flowers
and wear them in her hair!

Hasbro

08

my LITTLE
PONY

FRIENDSHIP
IS MAGIC

Hasbro

WWW.MYLITTLEPONY.COM

Name

Trixie Lulamoon

Description

Trixie Lulamoon is great at magic tricks!

TRADING CARD

TRIXIE LULAMOON™

is great at
magic tricks!

09

MY LITTLE PONY
FRIENDSHIP IS MAGIC

WWW.MYLITTLEPONY.COM

Pony Tribe
Unicorn

Cutie Mark
Moon and Wand

Eye Color
Purple

Hair Color
White

Color
Blue

Figure Style
Shimmer-Gem

Pony Tribe
Unicorn

Eye Color
Blue

Color
White

Cutie Mark
Three Stars

Hair Color
Purple

Figure Style
Shimmer-Gem

US Wave
2013 / 1

Figure
10

Name

Twilight Velvet

Description

Twilight Velvet loves writing stories about adventures!

TRADING CARD

TWILIGHT VELVET™

loves writing stories
about adventures!

10

MY LITTLE PONY

FRIENDSHIP IS MAGIC

WWW.MYLITTLEPONY.COM

NAME

MOSELY ORANGE

DESCRIPTION

Mosely Orange loves to have fancy parties!

TRADING CARD

MOSELY ORANGE™

loves to have fancy parties!

MY LITTLE PONY

FRIENDSHIP IS MAGIC

WWW.MYLITTLEPONY.COM

Eye Color
Blue

Hair Color
Green

Color
Yellow

Cutie Mark
Orange

Pony Tribe
Earth

Figure Style
Classic

Eye Color
Green

Hair Color
Yellow

Color
Purple

Cutie Mark
Two Bunches of
Green Grapes

Pony Tribe
Earth

Figure Style
Classic

NAME

BERRY GREEN

DESCRIPTION

Berry Green has lots of
friends she can always
count on!

TRADING CARD

BERRY GREEN™

has lots of friends she
can always count on!

MY LITTLE PONY
FRIENDSHIP IS MAGIC

WWW.MYLITTLEPONY.COM

US Wave
2013 / 1

Figure
13

NAME

MERRY MAY

DESCRIPTION

Merry May loves all flowers, especially spring daisies!

Hair Color
Light and Dark Purple

TRADING CARD

MERRY MAY™
loves all flowers, especially spring daisies!

13

WWW.MYLITTLEPONY.COM

Eye Color
Pink

Pony Tribe
Pegasus

Cutie Mark
Three Flowers

Color
Green

Figure Style
Classic

Pony Tribe
Unicorn

Eye Color
Green

Cutie Mark
Two Cherries

Color
Brown

Hair Color
Red

Figure Style
Classic

NAME

CHERRY SPICES

DESCRIPTION

Cherry Spices loves to bake
and make up yummy recipes!

TRADING CARD

CHERRY SPICES™
loves to bake and make
up yummy recipes!

14

MY LITTLE PONY
Friendship is MAGIC

WWW.MYLITTLEPONY.COM

123

US Wave
2013 / 1

Figure
15

NAME

ELECTRIC SKY

DESCRIPTION

Electric Sky has so many smart ideas to share!

TRADING CARD

ELECTRIC SKY™

has so many smart ideas to share!

15

Hasbro

MY LITTLE PONY

FRIENDSHIP IS MAGIC

Hasbro

WWW.MYLITTLEPONY.COM

Pony Tribe
Unicorn

Eye Color
Blue

Cutie Mark
Three Lightbulbs

Hair Color
Dark Blue

Color
Yellow

Figure Style
Classic

Hair Color
Green

Cutie Mark
Three Cupcakes

Eye Color
Green

Pony Tribe
Earth

Color
Pink

US Wave
2013 / 1

Figure
16

NAME

CRIMSON GALA

DESCRIPTION

Crimson Gala gives everyone
treats when she visits!

Figure Style
Classic

TRADING CARD

CRIMSON GALA™

gives everyone treats
when she visits!

16

Hasbro

MY LITTLE PONY
FRIENDSHIP IS MAGIC

WWW.MYLITTLEPONY.COM

Hasbro

125

Name

Amethyst Star

Description

Amethyst Star loves to dance when she hears music!

Hair Color
Purple

Pony Tribe
Unicorn

Cutie Mark
Three Diamonds

Eye Color
Purple

Color
Purple

Figure Style
Classic

Eye Color
Blue

Hair Color
Blue

Color
Gray

Cutie Mark
Three Stars

Pony Tribe
Earth

NAME

TWILIGHT SKY

DESCRIPTION

Twilight Sky loves to play guessing games with friends!

Figure Style
Classic

TRADING CARD

TWILIGHT SKY™
loves to play guessing
games with friends!

Hasbro

18

MY LITTLE PONY

FRIENDSHIP IS MAGIC

Hasbro

WWW.MYLITTLEPONY.COM

127

US Wave
2013 / 1

Figure
19

NAME

SASSAFLASH

DESCRIPTION

Sassaflash loves watching clouds blow across the sky!

TRADING CARD

SASSAFLASH™

loves watching clouds blow across the sky!

19

WWW.MYLITTLEPONY.COM

Hair Color
Yellow

Eye Color
Orange

Pony Tribe
Pegasus

Cutie Mark
Two Lightning Bolts

Color
Blue

Figure Style
Classic

Pony Tribe
Unicorn

Eye Color
Blue

Color
Blue

Cutie Mark
Magnet

Hair Color
Red

Figure Style
Classic

US Wave
2013 / 1

Figure
20

NAME

MAGNET BOLT

DESCRIPTION

Magnet Bolt attracts a lot of attention wherever she goes!

TRADING CARD

MAGNET BOLT™

attracts a lot of attention
wherever she goes!

20

WWW.MYLITTLEPONY.COM

US Wave
2013 / 1

Figure
21

Name

Royal Riff

Description

Royal Riff makes up songs to sing together with friends!

TRADING CARD

Eye Color
Orange

Hair Color
White

Color
Light Purple

Cutie Mark
Two Treble Clefs

Pony Tribe
Earth

Figure Style
Classic

130

Hair Color
Pink

Cutie Mark
Pie

Eye Color
Green

Color
Green

Pony Tribe
Earth

Figure Style
Classic

NAME

PEACHY SWEET

DESCRIPTION

Peachy Sweet is always smiling wherever she goes!

TRADING CARD

my LITTLE PONY
FRIENDSHIP IS MAGIC

PEACHY SWEET™

is always smiling
wherever she goes!

Hasbro

22

Hasbro

WWW.MYLITTLEPONY.COM

131

NAME

CHANCE-A-LOT

DESCRIPTION

Chance-A-Lot is always cheerful and trying new things!

Hair Color
Brown

Eye Color
Blue

Cutie Mark
Three Horseshoes

Color
Orange

Pony Tribe
Earth

Figure Style
Classic

TRADING CARD

CHANCE-A-LOT™
is always cheerful and trying new things!

23

WWW.MYLITTLEPONY.COM

Hair Color
Blue

Eye Color
Pink

Color
Blue

Cutie Mark
Two Horseshoes

Pony Tribe
Earth

Figure Style
Classic

NAME

SHOESHINE

DESCRIPTION

Shoeshine is understanding
and listens to her friends!

TRADING CARD

SHOESHINE™

is understanding and
listens to her friends!

24

MY LITTLE PONY
FRIENDSHIP IS MAGIC

WWW.MYLITTLEPONY.COM

133

BLIND BAG

PONY CHECKLIST

- ☐ Pinkie Pie
- ☐ Fluttershy
- ☐ Twilight Sparkle
- ☐ Rainbow Dash
- ☐ Rarity
- ☐ Applejack
- ☐ Cherry Pie
- ☐ Apple Fritter
- ☐ Banana Fluff
- ☐ Lilac Links
- ☐ Cherry Fizzy
- ☐ Misty Fly

- ☐ Banana Bliss
- ☐ Sweetie Drops
- ☐ Holly Dash
- ☐ Berry Dreams
- ☐ Soarin
- ☐ Lucky Clover
- ☐ Lily Blossom
- ☐ Apple Stars
- ☐ Barber Groomsby
- ☐ Caramel Apple
- ☐ Spitfire
- ☐ Lily Valley

Name

Pinkie Pie

Description

Pinkie Pie keeps her friends laughing and smiling all day!

TRADING CARD

PINKIE PIE®
keeps her friends laughing and smiling all day!

01

My Little Pony
FRIENDSHIP IS MAGIC

WWW.MYLITTLEPONY.COM

Hair Color
Pink

Cutie Mark
Three Balloons

Eye Color
Blue

Figure Style
Crystal-Shine

Color
Pink

Pony Tribe
Earth

Eye Color
Green

Hair Color
Pink

Pony Tribe
Pegasus

Color
Yellow

Cutie Mark
Three Butterflies

Figure Style
Crystal-Shine

US Wave
2013 / 2

Figure
2

NAME

FLUTTERSHY

DESCRIPTION

Fluttershy likes taking care of her friends!

TRADING CARD

FLUTTERSHY®

likes taking care of her friends!

02

my LITTLE PONY

FRIENDSHIP IS MAGIC

WWW.MYLITTLEPONY.COM

Hasbro

Name

Twilight Sparkle

Description

Twilight Sparkle loves learning with her friends!

TRADING CARD

TWILIGHT SPARKLE™

loves learning with her friends!

03

Pony Tribe
Unicorn

Cutie Mark
Pink Sparkle

Eye Color
Purple

Hair Color
Pink and Purple

Color
Purple

Figure Style
Crystal-Shine

Eye Color
Purple

Hair Color
Rainbow

Pony Tribe
Pegasus

Color
Blue

Cutie Mark
Rainbow Lightning Bolt

Figure Style
Crystal-Shine

US Wave
2013 / 2

Figure
4

NAME

RAINBOW DASH

DESCRIPTION

Rainbow Dash is always ready to help her friends!

TRADING CARD

RAINBOW DASH®

is always ready to
help her friends.

my LITTLE PONY

FRIENDSHIP IS MAGIC

Hasbro

04

WWW.MYLITTLEPONY.COM

NAME

RARITY

DESCRIPTION

Rarity loves to give her friends great advice!

TRADING CARD

RARITY®
loves to give her friends great advice!

05

MY LITTLE PONY
FRIENDSHIP IS MAGIC

WWW.MYLITTLEPONY.COM

Cutie Mark
Three Gems

Pony Tribe
Unicorn

Hair Color
Pink and Purple

Eye Color
Blue

Figure Style
Crystal-Shine

Color
White

Hair Color
Yellow

Eye Color
Green

Color
Orange

Cutie Mark
Three Apples

Figure Style
Crystal-Shine

Pony Tribe
Earth

US Wave
2013 / 2

Figure
6

NAME

APPLEJACK

DESCRIPTION

Applejack is honest, friendly and sweet to the core.

TRADING CARD

APPLEJACK™

is honest, friendly and sweet to the core!

06

MY LITTLE PONY

FRIENDSHIP IS MAGIC

WWW.MYLITTLEPONY.COM

141

NAME

CHERRY PIE

DESCRIPTION

Cherry Pie loves to bake for her friends!

TRADING CARD

CHERRY PIE™

loves to bake
for her friends!

07

my LITTLE PONY

FRIENDSHIP IS MAGIC

WWW.MYLITTLEPONY.COM

Pony Tribe
Unicorn

Cutie Mark
Cherry Pie

Eye Color
Blue

Hair Color
Orange and
Yellow

Color
Pink

Figure Style
Crystal-Shine

Hair Color
Green

Color
Yellow

Eye Color
Green

Cutie Mark
Three Apple
Fritters

Pony Tribe
Earth

Figure Style
Crystal-Shine

US Wave
2013 / 2

Figure
8

NAME

APPLE
FRITTER

DESCRIPTION

Apple Fritter loves to give
homemade gifts to her
friends!

TRADING
CARD

APPLE FRITTER
loves to give homemade
gifts to her friends!

MY LITTLE PONY
FRIENDSHIP IS MAGIC

WWW.MYLITTLEPONY.COM

143

Name

BANANA FLUFF

Description

Banana Fluff collects pretty
gems to make jewelry!

BANANA FLUFF™

collects pretty gems
to make jewelry!

Hasbro

09

my LITTLE PONY

FRIENDSHIP
IS MAGIC

Hasbro

WWW.MYLITTLEPONY.COM

Cutie Mark
Three Diamonds

Pony Tribe
Unicorn

Eye Color
Pink

Hair Color
Purple

Color
Yellow

Figure Style
Crystal-Shine

Hair Color
Blue

Cutie Mark
Two Horseshoes

US Wave
2013 / 2

Figure
10

Name

Lilac Links

Eye Color
Pink

Description

Lilac Links always wears a
good luck charm!

Figure Style
Crystal-Shine

Color
Purple

Pony Tribe
Earth

TRADING CARD

LILAC LINKS
always wears a
good luck charm!

Hasbro

10

MY LITTLE PONY

FRIENDSHIP
MAGIC

Hasbro

WWW.MYLITTLEPONY.COM

NAME

CHERRY FIZZY

DESCRIPTION

Cherry Fizzy loves to tell jokes and riddles to his friends!

TRADING CARD

CHERRY FIZZY™

loves to tell jokes and riddles to his friends!

11

Hasbro

my little
PONY
FRIENDSHIP
IS MAGIC

WWW.MYLITTLEPONY.COM

Hasbro

Eye Color
Green

Hair Color
Brown

Figure Style
Crystal-Shine

Cutie Mark
Two Cherries

Color
Tan

Pony Tribe
Earth

Hair Color
Blue

Pony Tribe
Pegasus

US Wave
2013 / 2

Figure
12

Name

MISTY FLY

Description

Misty Fly is a talented member of the WONDERBOLTS flying team!

Eye Color
Goggle
Gleam

Cutie Mark
Lightning Bolt

Color
Blue

Figure Style
Crystal-Shine

TRADING CARD

MISTY FLY™

is a talented member of the WONDERBOLTS™ flying team!

Hasbro

12

my LITTLE PONY

FRIENDSHIP IS MAGIC

Hasbro

WWW.MYLITTLEPONY.COM

NAME

BANANA BLISS

DESCRIPTION

Banana Bliss loves to dance—
on the ground and in the air!

TRADING CARD

BANANA BLISS™

loves to dance — on the
ground and in the air!

13

my LITTLE PONY
FRIENDSHIP IS MAGIC

WWW.MYLITTLEPONY.COM

Hair Color
Pink and Purple

Eye Color
Purple

Pony Tribe
Pegasus

Color
Teal

Cutie Mark
Two Bananas

Figure Style
Crystal-Shine

Hair Color
Blue and Pink

Eye Color
Blue

Color
White

Cutie Mark
Three Candies

Figure Style
Crystal-Shine

Pony Tribe
Earth

US Wave
2013 / 2

Figure
14

NAME

SWEETIE DROPS

DESCRIPTION

Sweetie Drops knows sharing treats makes them taste sweeter!

TRADING CARD

SWEETIE DROPS™

knows sharing treats makes them taste sweeter!

Hasbro

MY LITTLE PONY

FRIENDSHIP IS MAGIC

Hasbro

WWW.MYLITTLEPONY.COM

14

NAME

HOLLY DASH

DESCRIPTION

Holly Dash loves to skip, gallop, and run everywhere!

TRADING CARD

HOLLY DASH™

loves to skip, gallop, and run everywhere!

15

MY LITTLE PONY

FRIENDSHIP IS MAGIC

WWW.MYLITTLEPONY.COM

Pony Tribe
Unicorn

Cutie Mark
Strawberry

Eye Color
Blue

Hair Color
Yellow, Blue,
and Purple

Color
Pink

Figure Style
Crystal-Shine

Hair Color
Yellow

Eye Color
Pink

Color
Blue

Cutie Mark
Berries

Figure Style
Crystal-Shine

Pony Tribe
Earth

TRADING CARD

BERRY DREAMS™
loves playing games with
her friends in the park!

my **LITTLE PONY**

FRIENDSHIP IS MAGIC

WWW.MYLITTLEPONY.COM

16

Hasbro

US Wave
2013 / 2

Figure
16

NAME

BERRY DREAMS

DESCRIPTION

Berry Dreams loves playing
games with her friends in
the park!

151

Name

SOARIN

Description

Soarin is the captain of the
WONDERBOLTS flying team!

Hair Color
Dark Blue

Pony Tribe
Pegasus

Eye Color
Goggle
Gleam

Cutie Mark
Winged
Lightning Bolt

Color
Blue

Figure Style
Crystal-Shine

152

Hair Color
Dark Gray

Figure Style
Crystal-Shine

Eye Color
Blue

Cutie Mark
Three Clovers

Color
Gray

Pony Tribe
Earth

US Wave
2013 / 2

Figure
18

NAME

LUCKY CLOVER

DESCRIPTION

Lucky Clover knows working together makes any job easier!

TRADING CARD

LUCKY CLOVER™

knows working makes any job easier!

my LITTLE PONY

FRIENDSHIP IS MAGIC

WWW.MYLITTLEPONY.COM

18

153

US Wave 2013 / 2   Figure 19

NAME

LILY BLOSSOM

DESCRIPTION

Lily Blossom is known for being graceful all the time!

TRADING CARD

LILY BLOSSOM™
is known for being graceful all the time!

Hasbro

19

my LITTLE PONY
FRIENDSHIP IS MAGIC

Hasbro

WWW.MYLITTLEPONY.COM

Eye Color
Purple

Hair Color
Yellow

Pony Tribe
Pegasus

Color
Purple

Cutie Mark
Three Lilies

Figure Style
Crystal-Shine

Cutie Mark
Two Apples

Pony Tribe
Unicorn

Hair Color
Green

Eye Color
Pink

Color
Purple

Figure Style
Crystal-Shine

NAME

APPLE STARS

DESCRIPTION

Apple Stars loves to spend
time talking with her friends!

TRADING
CARD

APPLE STARS™

loves to spend time
talking with her friends!

Hasbro

20

MY LITTLE PONY
FRIENDSHIP IS MAGIC

WWW.MYLITTLEPONY.COM

Hasbro

US Wave
2013 / 2

Figure
21

Name

BARBER
GROOMSBY

Description

Barber Groomsby makes sure
everypony's mane looks great!

TRADING CARD

BARBER GROOMSBY™
makes sure everypony's
mane looks great!

21

my LITTLE
PONY
FRIENDSHIP IS MAGIC

WWW.MYLITTLEPONY.COM

Eye Color
Blue

Hair Color
Brown

Figure Style
Crystal-Shine

Cutie Mark
Scissors and
Comb

Color
White

Pony Tribe
Earth

Hair Color
Yellow

Cutie Mark
Three Caramel Apples

Eye Color
Green

Color
Light Orange

Figure Style
Crystal-Shine

Pony Tribe
Earth

NAME

CARAMEL APPLE

DESCRIPTION

Caramel Apple loves to watch movies with her friends!

TRADING CARD

CARAMEL APPLE™
loves to watch movies with her friends!

22

MY LITTLE PONY
FRIENDSHIP IS MAGIC

Hasbro

WWW.MYLITTLEPONY.COM

Name

SPITFIRE

Description

Spitfire is a speedy member of the WONDERBOLTS flying team!

Hair Color
Orange and Yellow

SPITFIRE™

is a speedy member of the
WONDERBOLTS™ flying team!

WWW.MYLITTLEPONY.COM

Pony Tribe
Pegasus

Cutie Mark
Lightning Bolt

Eye Color
Goggle
Gleam

Color
Blue

Figure Style
Crystal-Shine

Hair Color
Yellow

Eye Color
Orange

Color
Pink

Cutie Mark
Three Lilies

Pony Tribe
Earth

Figure Style
Crystal-Shine

NAME

LILY VALLEY

DESCRIPTION

Lily Valley loves to be in the center of the action!

TRADING CARD

LILY VALLEY™
loves to be in the center of the action!

Hasbro

24

my LITTLE PONY

FRIENDSHIP IS MAGIC

Hasbro

WWW.MYLITTLEPONY.COM

BLiND BAG

PONY CHECKLIST

- ☐ Applejack
- ☐ Big McIntosh
- ☐ Royal Riff
- ☐ Mosely Orange
- ☐ Gilda the Griffon
- ☐ Flam
- ☐ Flim Skim
- ☐ Fluttershy
- ☐ Skywishes
- ☐ Granny Smith
- ☐ Princess Cadance
- ☐ Golden Harvest
- ☐ Flower Wishes
- ☐ Pinkie Pie
- ☐ Sassaflash
- ☐ Comet Tail
- ☐ Rainbow Dash
- ☐ Sunny Rays
- ☐ Gardenia Glow
- ☐ Lemon Hearts
- ☐ Rarity
- ☐ Ribbon Wishes
- ☐ Lotus Blossom
- ☐ Twilight Sparkle

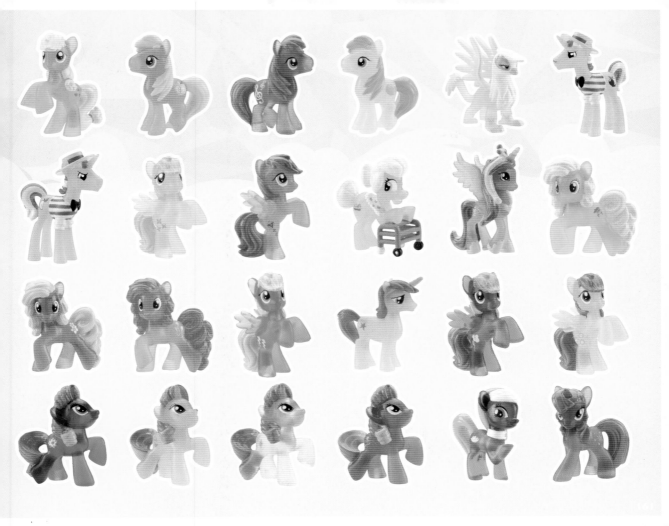

Name

APPLEJACK

Description

Applejack is honest, friendly and sweet to the core!

TRADING CARD

APPLE JACK
is honest, friendly and sweet to the core!

01

WWW.MYLITTLEPONY.COM

Eye Color
Green

Hair Color
Yellow

Cutie Mark
Three Apples

Color
Orange

Pony Tribe
Earth

Figure Style
Neon-Bright

Eye Color
Green

Hair Color
Orange

Color
Red

Cutie Mark
Apple

Pony Tribe
Earth

Figure Style
Neon-Bright

US Wave
2013 / 3

Figure
2

NAME

BIG McINTOSH

DESCRIPTION

Big McIntosh is a very gentle and wise pony!

TRADING CARD

BIG McINTOSH™

is a very gentle and wise pony!

my little PONY
FRIENDSHIP IS MAGIC

WWW.MYLITTLEPONY.COM

163

Name

Royal Riff

Description

Royal Riff makes up songs to sing together with friends!

TRADING CARD

ROYAL RIFF
makes up songs to sing
together with friends!

03

WWW.MYLITTLEPONY.COM

Hair Color
Pink

Color
Light Purple

Cutie Mark
Two Treble Clefs

Eye Color
Brown

Figure Style
Neon-Bright

Pony Tribe
Earth

Eye Color
Blue

Hair Color
Green

Color
Yellow

Cutie Mark
Orange

Pony Tribe
Earth

Figure Style
Neon-Bright

NAME

MOSELY ORANGE

DESCRIPTION

Mosely Orange loves to have fancy parties!

TRADING CARD

MOSELY ORANGE

loves to have fancy parties!

Hasbro

04

MY LITTLE PONY
FRIENDSHIP IS MAGIC

WWW.MYLITTLEPONY.COM

Hasbro

NAME

GILDA THE GRIFFON

DESCRIPTION

Gilda the Griffon loves flying with Rainbow Dash!

TRADING CARD

GILDA THE GRIFFON

loves flying with
RAINBOW DASH!

05

MY LITTLE PONY

FRIENDSHIP IS MAGIC

WWW.MYLITTLEPONY.COM

Figure Style
Neon-Bright

Eye Color
Purple

Color
Brown and White

Pony Tribe
Unicorn

Eye Color
Green

Hair Color
Red and White

Color
Green

Figure Style
Neon-Bright

Cutie Mark
Cut Apple

NAME

FLAM

DESCRIPTION

Flam of the Flim Flam
Brothers loves apple cider!

TRADING CARD

FLAM™

of the Flim Flam Brothers
loves apple cider!

Hasbro

06

MY LITTLE PONY
FRIENDSHIP IS MAGIC

Hasbro

WWW.MYLITTLEPONY.COM

NAME

FLIM SKIM

DESCRIPTION

Flim Skim of the Flim Flam
Brothers loves to sing!

FLIM SKIM
of the Flim Flam
Brothers
loves to sing!

07

WWW.MYLITTLEPONY.COM

Eye Color
Green

Cutie Mark
Apple Slice

Pony Tribe
Unicorn

Color
Green

Hair Color
Red and White

Figure Style
Neon-Bright

Eye Color
Green

Hair Color
Pink

Pony Tribe
Pegasus

Color
Yellow

Cutie Mark
Three Butterflies

Figure Style
Neon-Bright

NAME

FLUTTERSHY

DESCRIPTION

Fluttershy likes taking care of her friends!

TRADING CARD

FLUTTERSHY®
likes taking care of
her friends!

MY LITTLE PONY
friendship is magic

WWW.MYLITTLEPONY.COM

US Wave
2013 / 3

Figure
9

Name

Skywishes

Description

Skywishes has big dreams and never gives up!

TRADING CARD

SKYWISHES™

has big dreams and
never gives up!

09

my LITTLE PONY

Fairytale Tales

WWW.MYLITTLEPONY.COM

Eye Color
Green

Hair Color
Pink and Purple

Pony Tribe
Pegasus

Color
Pink

Cutie Mark
Kite

Figure Style
Neon-Bright

170

Hair Color
White

Eye Color
Orange

Cutie Mark
Pie

Color
Green

Pony Tribe
Earth

Figure Style
Neon-Bright

NAME

GRANNY
SMITH

DESCRIPTION

Granny Smith is famous for
baking apple pies!

TRADING
CARD

GRANNY SMITH™

is famous for baking apple pies!

MY LITTLE PONY
FRIENDSHIP IS MAGIC

WWW.MYLITTLEPONY.COM

10

Name

Princess Cadance

Description

Princess Cadance likes to spend time helping others.

TRADING CARD

PRINCESS CADANCE™

likes to spend time helping others.

WWW.MYLITTLEPONY.COM

Pony Tribe
Pegasus Unicorn

Eye Color
Purple

Cutie Mark
Crystal Heart

Color
Pink

Hair Color
Purple, Pink, and Yellow

Figure Style
Neon-Bright

Hair Color
Yellow

Cutie Mark
Two Carrots

Eye Color
Green

Color
Orange

Figure Style
Neon-Bright

Pony Tribe
Earth

TRADING CARD

GOLDEN HARVEST™
loves sharing treats from the garden!

Hasbro 12

MY LITTLE PONY
Friendship is Magic

WWW.MYLITTLEPONY.COM

NAME

GOLDEN HARVEST

DESCRIPTION

Golden Harvest loves sharing treats from the garden!

Name

Flower Wishes

Description

Flower Wishes grows flowers in every color of the rainbow!

Hair Color
Green

Cutie Mark
Two Flowers

Eye Color
Green

Figure Style
Neon-Bright

Color
Pink

Pony Tribe
Earth

TRADING CARD

FLOWER WISHES™
grows flowers in every color of the rainbow!

13

my little PONY
FRIENDSHIP IS MAGIC

WWW.MYLITTLEPONY.COM

Hair Color
Pink

Cutie Mark
Three Balloons

Eye Color
Blue

Color
Pink

Figure Style
Neon-Bright

Pony Tribe
Earth

NAME

PINKIE PIE

DESCRIPTION

Pinkie Pie keeps her friends
laughing and smiling all day!

TRADING CARD

PINKIE PIE®

keeps her friends laughing
and smiling all day!

14

WWW.MYLITTLEPONY.COM

US Wave
2013 / 3

Figure
15

NAME

SASSAFLASH

DESCRIPTION

Sassaflash loves watching
clouds blow across the sky!

TRADING CARD

SASSAFLASH™

loves watching clouds
blow across the sky!

15

WWW.MYLITTLEPONY.COM

Eye Color
Orange

Hair Color
Yellow

Pony Tribe
Pegasus

Color
Green

Cutie Mark
Two Lightning
Bolts

Figure Style
Neon-Bright

Pony Tribe
Unicorn

Cutie Mark
Shooting Star

Hair Color
Blue

Eye Color
Blue

Color
Yellow

Figure Style
Neon-Bright

Name

Comet Tail

Description

Comet Tail runs so fast that
he looks like a shooting star!

TRADING CARD

COMET TAIL™

runs so fast that he looks
like a shooting star!

16

MY LITTLE PONY
FRIENDSHIP IS MAGIC

WWW.MYLITTLEPONY.COM

Name

Rainbow Dash

Description

Rainbow Dash is always ready to help her friends!

TRADING CARD

RAINBOW DASH®
is always ready to help her friends!

17

Eye Color
Pink

Hair Color
Rainbow

Color
Blue

Pony Tribe
Pegasus

Figure Style
Neon-Bright

Cutie Mark
Rainbow
Lightning Bolt

WWW.MYLITTLEPONY.COM

Eye Color
Purple

Hair Color
Pink and Purple

Pony Tribe
Pegasus

Color
Yellow

Cutie Mark
Three Suns

Figure Style
Neon-Bright

Name

SUNNY RAYS

Description

Sunny Rays has a lot of bright ideas to share.

TRADING CARD

SUNNY RAYS™

has a lot of bright ideas to share.

Hasbro

18

MY LITTLE PONY

FRIENDSHIP IS MAGIC

Hasbro

WWW.MYLITTLEPONY.COM

US Wave
2013 / 3

Figure
19

NAME

GARDENIA GLOW

DESCRIPTION

Gardenia Glow knows how to make a garden grow!

GARDENIA GLOW

knows how to make a garden grow!

19

Hair Color
Pink

Eye Color
Blue

Cutie Mark
Flower

Figure Style
Neon-Bright

Color
Blue

Pony Tribe
Unicorn

WWW.MYLITTLEPONY.COM

Hair Color
Blue

Pony Tribe
Unicorn

Cutie Mark
Three Hearts

Eye Color
Purple

Color
Yellow

Figure Style
Neon-Bright

NAME

LEMON HEARTS

DESCRIPTION

Lemon Hearts always takes
time to show she cares!

TRADING CARD

LEMON HEARTS

always takes time to
show she cares!

20

MY LITTLE PONY
FRIENDSHIP IS MAGIC

WWW.MYLITTLEPONY.COM

Name

RARITY

Description

Rarity loves to give her friends
great advice!

TRADING
CARD

RARITY®

loves to give her friends
great advice!

21

WWW.MYLITTLEPONY.COM

Eye Color
Blue

Pony Tribe
Unicorn

Cutie Mark
Three Gems

Figure Style
Neon-Bright

Hair Color
Pink and Purple

Color
White

Hair Color
Blue and Purple

Pony Tribe
Unicorn

Cutie Mark
Wand and Stars

Eye Color
Blue

Color
Dark Pink

Figure Style
Neon-Bright

NAME

RIBBON WISHES

DESCRIPTION

Ribbon Wishes loves to wish on shooting stars!

TRADING CARD

RIBBON WISHES™

loves to wish on shooting stars!

22

WWW.MYLITTLEPONY.COM

183

Name

LOTUS BLOSSOM

Description

Lotus Blossom helps her friends feel calm and relaxed!

Hair Color
Pink with White Headband

Eye Color
Blue

Cutie Mark
Lotus

Figure Style
Neon-Bright

Pony Tribe
Earth

Color
Blue

Pony Tribe
Unicorn

Eye Color
Purple

Color
Purple

Cutie Mark
Pink Sparkle

Hair Color
Pink and Purple

Figure Style
Neon-Bright

NAME

TWILIGHT SPARKLE

DESCRIPTION

Twilight Sparkle loves learning with her friends!

TRADING CARD

TWILIGHT SPARKLE

loves learning with her friends!

24

MY LITTLE PONY
FRIENDSHIP IS MAGIC

WWW.MYLITTLEPONY.COM

EUROPEAN BLIND BAGS

STAR SWIRL

Star Swirl always
sparkles!

PONY CHECKLIST

- ☐ Star Swirl
- ☐ Tealove
- ☐ Ribbon Heart
- ☐ Daisy Dream
- ☐ Stardash
- ☐ Honeybelle
- ☐ Rainbow Flash
- ☐ Pudding Pie

TEALOVE

Tealove loves
cozy chats!

RIBBON HEART

Ribbon Heart is
always ready to play!

DAISY DREAM

Daisy Dream is fresh as a daisy!

STARDASH

Stardash loves shooting stars!

RAINBOW FLASH

Rainbow Flash loves bright colors!

HONEYBELLE

Honeybelle loves to visit friends!

PUDDING PIE

Pudding Pie loves sharing with friends!

THREE-CHARACTER COLLECTOR SETS

2012–Spring 2013 Mini Collections

PONY CHECKLISTS

□ **PONY WEDDING**
- Shining Armor
- Princess Cadance
- Twilight Sparkle

□ **CLOUDSDALE**
- Rainbow Dash
- Gilda the Griffon
- Wonderbolts pony

□ **APPLE FAMILY**
- Granny Smith
- Big McIntosh
- Applejack

□ **SPA PONY**
- Lotus Blossom
- Zecora
- Pinkie Pie

□ **CLASS OF CUTIE MARKS**
- Diamond Dazzle Tiara
- Apple Bloom
- Applejack

□ **FAMOUS FRIENDS**
- Rarity
- Photo Finish
- Hoity Toity

SET NAME

PONY WEDDING

CHARACTERS INCLUDED

Shining Armor
Princess Cadance
Twilight Sparkle

BACKGROUND

Palace

TWILIGHT SPARKLE

The burden of keeping Canterlot safe and secure rests squarely on my shoulders.

My love will give you strength.

SHINING ARMOR

PRINCESS CADANCE

Don't you know how to take "Get lost" for an answer?!

GILDA THE GRIFFON

WONDERBOLTS PONY

RAINBOW DASH

SET NAME

CLOUDSDALE

CHARACTERS INCLUDED
Rainbow Dash
Gilda the Griffon
Wonderbolts pony

BACKGROUND
Cloudsdale

SET NAME

APPLE FAMILY

CHARACTERS INCLUDED

Granny Smith
Big McIntosh
Applejack

BACKGROUND

Sweet Apple Acres

BIG McINTOSH

APPLEJACK

YEE-HAW!

GRANNY SMITH

LOTUS BLOSSOM

PINKIE PIE

ZECORA

I have just the trick that will fix you up quite quick.

US
2013

SET NAME

SPA PONY

CHARACTERS INCLUDED

Lotus Blossom
Zecora
Pinkie Pie

BACKGROUND

Spa

SET NAME

CLASS OF CUTIE MARKS

CHARACTERS INCLUDED

Diamond Dazzle Tiara
Apple Bloom
Applejack

BACKGROUND

Ponyville

RARITY

PHOTO FINISH

I go.

Oh, this can't be the same designer.

HOITY TOITY

US
2013

SET NAME

FAMOUS FRIENDS

CHARACTERS INCLUDED

Rarity
Photo Finish
Hoity Toity

BACKGROUND

Fashion show dressing room

THREE-CHARACTER COLLECTOR SETS

Fall 2013 Mini Collections

PONY CHECKLISTS

☐ **PONY LESSON**
  Silver Spoon
  Twist-a-loo
  Cheerilee

☐ **ROYAL SURPRISE**
  Queen Chrysalis
  Princess Celestia
  Twilight Sparkle

☐ **GROOVIN' HOOVES**
  Octavia Melody
  Lyra Heartstrings
  Lyrica Lilac

Set Name

Pony Lesson

Characters Included

Silver Spoon
Twist-a-loo
Cheerilee

Background

School

I love being special.

Silver Spoon

TWIST-A-LOO

All right, my little ponies,
time for class!

CHEERILEE

Set Name

Royal Surprise

Characters Included

Queen Chrysalis
Princess Celestia
Twilight Sparkle

Background

Palace

Equestria has more love than any place I've ever encountered.

QUEEN CHRYSALIS

TWILIGHT SPARKLE

PRINCESS CELESTIA

Set Name

Groovin' Hooves

Characters Included

Octavia Melody
Lyra Heartstrings
Lyrica Lilac

Background

Park

Octavia Melody

I love them.

LYRA HEARTSTRINGS

LYRICA LILAC

MULTI-CHARACTER COLLECTOR SETS

2013 Deluxe Mini Collections

PONY CHECKLISTS

☐ **CAKE FAMILY BABYSITTING FUN**
- Pinkie Pie
- Pumpkin Cake
- Pound Cake
- Nurse Redheart
- Mrs. Dazzle Cake
- Mr. Carrot Cake

☐ **ELEMENTS OF HARMONY FRIENDS**
- Nightmare Moon
- Manny Roar
- Rarity
- Fluttershy
- Steven Magnet

SET NAME

CAKE FAMILY BABYSITTING FUN

CHARACTERS INCLUDED

Pinkie Pie
Pumpkin Cake
Pound Cake
Nurse Redheart
Mrs. Dazzle Cake
Mr. Carrot Cake

BACKGROUND

Cake family house

NURSE REDHEART

Shhh. The babies are trying to sleep.

PINKIE PIE

MRS. DAZZLE CAKE

MR. CARROT CAKE

PUMPKIN CAKE

POUND CAKE

Set Name

Elements of Harmony Friends

Characters Included

Nightmare Moon
Manny Roar
Rarity
Fluttershy
Steven Magnet

Background

Ponyville

Manny Roar

Nightmare Moon

RARITY

Sometimes we all just need to be shown a little kindness.

FLUTTERSHY

STEVEN MAGNET

RETAILER EXCLUSIVES

2011: Toys"R"Us

PONY CHECKLIST

☐ **PONY COLLECTION**

Pinkie Pie

Applejack

Rainbow Dash

Rarity

Twilight Sparkle

Fluttershy

Coconut Cream

Sweetsong

Skywishes

Gardenia Glow

Beachberry

Peachy Pie

Figure
I

NAME

PINKIE PIE

DESCRIPTION

Pinkie Pie keeps her pony
friends laughing and smiling
all day! Cheerful and playful,
she always looks on the
bright side.

TRADING CARD

PINKIE PIE keeps
her pony friends laughing
and smiling all day! Cheerful
and playful, she always looks
on the bright side.

Eye Color
Blue

Hair Color
Dark Pink

Cutie Mark
Three Balloons

Color
Pink

Figure Style
Classic

Pony Tribe
Earth

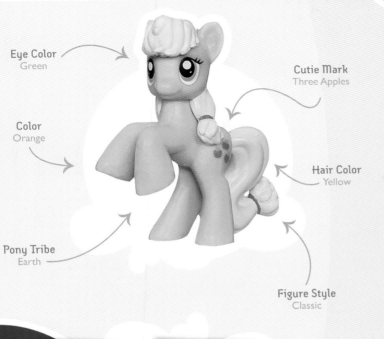

Eye Color
Green

Color
Orange

Pony Tribe
Earth

Cutie Mark
Three Apples

Hair Color
Yellow

Figure Style
Classic

NAME

APPLEJACK

DESCRIPTION

Applejack is honest, friendly and sweet to the core! She loves to be outside, and her friends know they can always count on her.

TRADING CARD

APPLEJACK is honest, friendly and sweet to the core! She loves to be outside, and her friends know they can always count on her.

Name

Rainbow Dash

Description

Rainbow Dash loves to fly as fast as she can! She is always ready to play a game, go on an adventure, or help out one of her friends.

TRADING CARD

RAINBOW DASH
loves to fly as fast as she can! She is always ready to play a game, go on an adventure, or help out one of her friends.

Eye Color
Purple

Pony Tribe
Pegasus

Hair Color
Rainbow

Cutie Mark
Rainbow
Lightning Bolt

Color
Blue

Figure Style
Classic

Pony Tribe
Unicorn

Eye Color
Blue

Hair Color
Pink and Purple

Color
White

Cutie Mark
Three Gems

Figure Style
Classic

2011
Toys"R"Us

Figure
4

Name

RARITY

DESCRIPTION

Rarity knows how to add sparkle to any outfit! She loves to give her friends advice on the latest pony fashions and hairstyles.

TRADING CARD

MY LITTLE PONY

RARITY™ knows how to add sparkle to any outfit! She loves to give her friends advice on the latest pony fashions and hairstyles.

Rarity

Hasbro

Name

Twilight Sparkle

Description

Twilight Sparkle tries to find the answer to every question! Whether studying a book or spending time with friends, she always learns something new!

TRADING CARD

TWILIGHT SPARKLE tries to find the answer to every question! Whether studying a book or spending time with friends, she always learns something new!

Eye Color
Purple

Pony Tribe
Unicorn

Cutie Mark
Pink Sparkle

Color
Purple

Figure Style
Classic

Hair Color
Pink and Purple

Hair Color
Pink

Eye Color
Green

Pony Tribe
Pegasus

Cutie Mark
Three Butterflies

Color
Yellow

Figure Style
Classic

2011
Toys"R"Us

Figure
6

NAME

FLUTTERSHY

DESCRIPTION

Fluttershy is a kind and gentle pony with a big heart. She likes to take care of others, especially her little animal friends!

TRADING CARD

my LITTLE PONY

FLUTTERSHY®
is a kind and gentle pony
with a big heart. She likes to
take care of others, especially
her little animal friends!

6

217

NAME

COCONUT CREAM

DESCRIPTION

Coconut Cream makes delicious pies to share at parties and picnics. The only thing she won't share is the secret ingredient!

Hair Color
Yellow, Pink, and Green

Eye Color
Blue

Cutie Mark
Pie

Color
White

Pony Tribe
Earth

Figure Style
Classic

Hair Color
Pink

Eye Color
Blue

Pony Tribe
Pegasus

Cutie Mark
Guitar

Color
Purple

Figure Style
Classic

NAME

SWEETSONG

DESCRIPTION

Sweetsong has a beautiful voice! She loves singing songs for her friends, especially when they sing along.

TRADING CARD

MY LITTLE PONY

SWEETSONG™
has a beautiful voice! She loves singing songs for her friends, especially when they sing along.

SWEETSONG™

Hasbro

Hasbro

8

Name

Skywishes

Description

Skywishes has big dreams and never gives up. She loves wishing on stars, especially for her friends!

TRADING CARD

My Little Pony

SKYWISHES has big dreams and never gives up. She loves wishing on stars, especially for her friends!

Hasbro

SKYWISHES

9

Hair Color
Pink and Purple

Pony Tribe
Pegasus

Eye Color
Green

Color
Pink

Cutie Mark
Kite

Figure Style
Classic

Pony Tribe
Unicorn

Hair Color
Pink

Cutie Mark
Flower

Eye Color
Blue

Color
Green

Figure Style
Classic

NAME

GARDENIA GLOW

DESCRIPTION

Gardenia Glow knows how to make any garden grow! All it takes is a little love and care, and some help from her friends.

TRADING CARD

my LITTLE PONY

GARDENIA GLOW

Hasbro

GARDENIA GLOW™
knows how to make any garden grow! All it takes is a little love and care, and some help from her friends.

Hasbro

10

21

Toys"R"Us

Figure
11

NAME

BEACHBERRY

DESCRIPTION

Beachberry loves spending time at the beach! Soaking up sunshine and relaxing with her friends, she always has a great time!

Eye Color
Green

Pony Tribe
Unicorn

Cutie Mark
Flower

Color
Pink

Figure Style
Classic

Hair Color
Purple, Pink, and Orange

TRADING CARD

Eye Color
Green

Hair Color
Orange

Color
Orange

Cutie Mark
Peach

Figure Style
Classic

Pony Tribe
Earth

NAME

PEACHY PIE

DESCRIPTION

Peachy Pie loves baking sweet treats for her friends! She's always testing out new recipes for them to try.

TRADING CARD

my LITTLE PONY

PEACHY PIE

PEACHY PIE™
loves baking sweet treats for her friends! She's always testing out new recipes for them to try.

Hasbro

12

RETAILER EXCLUSIVES

2012:
Toys"R"Us
Walmart
Target

PONY CHECKLISTS

☐ **TOYS"R"US:**
FRIENDSHIP
CELEBRATION
COLLECTION

Sweetie Swirl

Firecracker Burst

Lily Blossom

Bumblesweet

Lemon Hearts

Pepperdance

Sugar Grape

Lulu Luck

Rainbow Flash

Sweetie Blue

Blossomforth

Flower Wishes

☐ **WALMART:**
PINKIE PIE & FRIENDS
MINI COLLECTION

Rainbow Dash

Pinkie Pie

Kiwi Tart

Seascape

Star Dasher

Dainty Daisy

Periwinkle

Applejack

Rarity

Waterfire

Pick-a-Lily

Rainbow Swirl

☐ **TARGET:**
PONY RAINBOW
COLLECTION

Pinkie Pie

Applejack

Fluttershy

Emerald Ray

Rainbow Dash

Twilight Sparkle

Rarity

My Little Pony Friendship is Magic
PINKIE PIE & FRIENDS Mini Collection
Only at Walmart
Includes 12 Ponies!
PONY POWER

My Little Pony Friendship is Magic
Includes stickers!
PONY RAINBOW COLLECTION
ONLY AT Target
CRYSTAL

My Little Pony Friendship is Magic
WARNING
FRIENDSHIP CELEBRATION COLLECTION

Friendship Celebration Collection

The ponies find special ways to share time together. They are Pony Friends Forever!

Sweetie Swirl and Firecracker Burst have a pizza party!

Lily Blossom and Bumblesweet go on a picnic outside!

Lemon Hearts and Pepperdance play together in a band!

226

Sugar Grape and Lulu Luck read stories at their sleepover!

Rainbow Flash and Sweetie Blue have fun at a birthday party!

Blossomforth and Flower Wishes have a tea party for two!

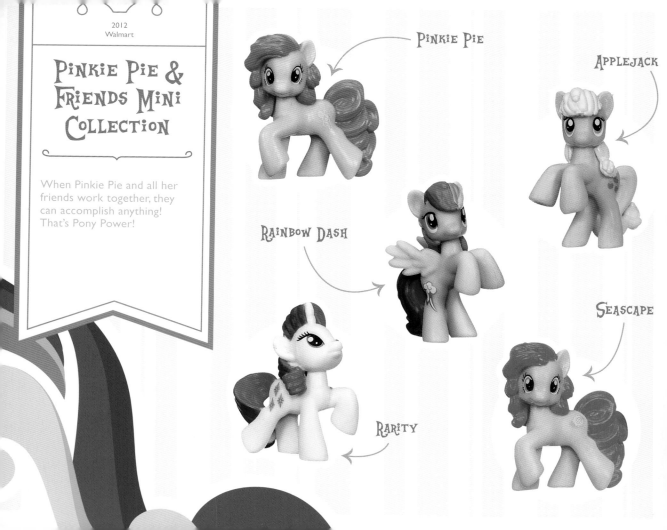

2012
Walmart

Pinkie Pie & Friends Mini Collection

When Pinkie Pie and all her friends work together, they can accomplish anything! That's Pony Power!

Pinkie Pie

Applejack

Rainbow Dash

Seascape

Rarity

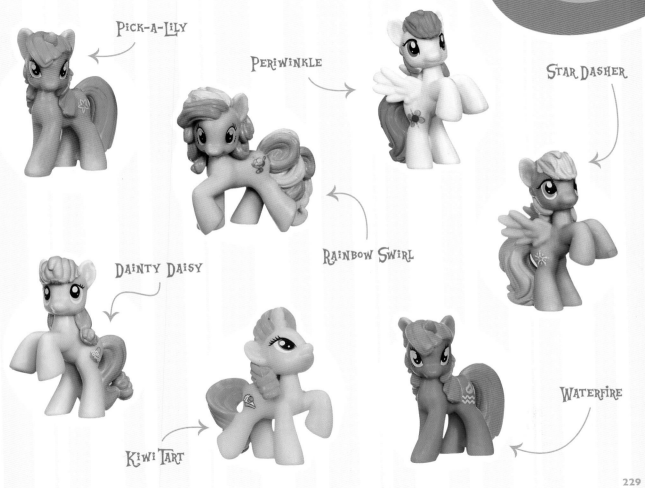

PICK-A-LILY

PERIWINKLE

STAR DASHER

RAINBOW SWIRL

DAINTY DAISY

KIWI TART

WATERFIRE

Pony Rainbow Collection

Welcome to the Crystal Empire, a magical place full of hidden secrets! The ponies shine and sparkle here!

Pinkie Pie

Applejack

Fluttershy